I0593747

Copyright © 2023 by Tansy Rayner Roberts

Cover art ©2023 Teresa Conner of Wolfsparrow Covers

Editorial services by Earl Grey Editing

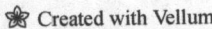 Created with Vellum

PRACTICAL WITCHING

TANSY RAYNER ROBERTS

CONTENTS

UNTITLED CRYPTID ALBUM

1. swinging on a star is definitely a safety hazard   3
2. moonbeams in a jar may be closer than they appear   6
3. wouldn't everyone rather be a fish?   10
4. play 'among the stars', it's my favourite   14
5. you can fly me to the moon but you can't make me drink   19
6. in other words   24

THE YEAR OF CRITICAL ROLLS

1. The Year of Viola   31
2. The Year of Mei   39
3. The Year of Jules   52
4. The Year of Viola   64
5. The Year of Juniper   74
6. The Year of Holly   89
7. The Year of Sage   95
8. The Year of Ferd   113
9. Back to Viola   123
10. The Year of Hebe   127
11. The Night of Sage   142
12. Happy New Year, Witches   146

LIKE WITCHES FOR COFFEE

1. Fake Geek Girl vs the Purple Couch of Sirenity   159
2. Fake Geek Girl vs the Dragonator   161
3. Fake Geek Girl vs Witchstarter   163
4. Fake Geek Girl vs Songs About Your Relationship Status   167
5. Fake Geek Girl vs Guest Instrumentals   172
6. Fake Geek Girl Vs The Basilisk Song   176
7. Fake Geek Girl Vs Medusa   180

8. Fake Geek Girl vs Everyone's Kissed The
   Drummer   182
9. Fake Geek Girl vs Cauldron Full of Cats   185
10. Fake Geek Girl Live in Concert (Witchstarter
    Exclusive)   188
11. Fake Geek Girl vs One True Pairings   194
12. Fake Geek Girl vs Belladonna U   205

BONUS PLAYLISTS AND EXTRAS

PART ONE
PREVIOUS HITS

Generic Love Song (Something About Spoilers)   211
Stupid Songs About Victorian Novels   215
Burn Hard   219

PART TWO
LIKE WITCHES FOR COFFEE: THE ALBUM

Cauldron Full of Cats   223
The Basilisk Song   227
Cryptids   231
Pockets   233
My T-Shirt's In Paris Now   237
Coffee is The Key To Surviving You   239

About the Author   241
Also by Tansy Rayner Roberts   243

UNTITLED CRYPTID
ALBUM

CHAPTER ONE

SWINGING ON A STAR IS DEFINITELY A SAFETY HAZARD

By the third day, the contestants were all starting to blur into each other, and Holly was starting to blur into her desk. She couldn't tell where she ended and this crisp white-topped surface began.

She only asked them three questions.

First: their name, which she checked off a list.

Second: "Do you have any equipment or magical needs we should be aware of?"

This was the most important question. For many performers, musical talent was entwined with their magical abilities. Those with what the industry referred to as 'the siren touch,' required their magic to be smooth, unglitching and accessible, to perform to the best of their ability.

Which was fine except that tech hates magic.

Cameras, microphones, lights, electrical instruments… if the contestant required magic on set, then Production needed to know in advance. There were ways to get around the problem: batteries packed with salt, bound with ceremonial cords and sigils, protective charms on everything, the judicious application of a vanilla latte.

In her old life, this behind the scenes shit was someone else's job. As the lead singer of Belladonna U's most popular local indie band, Holly had sung her brains out every Friday night without giving a second thought to whether she was going to fry the pub's wiring, or blow up the musical festival (in the not-cool way).

That was yesterday. Last month. A thousand years ago. Today, she was a (blah) grown up, doing a grown up (blah) job, and 99% of that job was to ask three questions of a slow-moving queue of wannabe pop stars.

The third question, the one that she hated most, reflected the attitude of the show. The contestants would be asked it again, once the cameras were rolling, by one of the bitchy C-grade celebrities on Talent Staff, or by Campion himself, the smooth-tongued host in his array of designer suits.

For now, it was Holly's job to weed out those few special snowflakes who had prepared a decent answer for the question instead of the same old, same old.

Third question: "What makes you special?"

Sometimes, the contestant crumpled. Sometimes, they were lost for words. Sometimes (rarely) they thought about it for a beat or two, and came up with something halfway interesting. Without exception, the ones who answered straight away without a moment of hesitation always said basically the same thing.

"I want to be a star."

"I really wannabe a star."

"I want it, you know? I really want it."

"I'm gonna be a star."

These should be her people. The people she most wanted to share a drink and a laugh with. Holly had spent the last three years with "I'm gonna be a star" rattling around in her head every time she picked up a mike or recoloured her hair or heard one of her own songs playing on campus radio, or saw the viewer numbers of their latest YouTube video roll upwards.

But she'd been weeding out Star Magic hopefuls for days now. Holly didn't feel like these were her people any more. She felt burnt out and cynical and kind of mean about the whole thing.

What was a star, anyway? What did it mean, to be famous for being yourself as hard as possible while everyone watched you do it? What did it mean, to be the person trying to find such a creature in the wild?

She might as well hunt cryptids: unicorns and bunyips and magical creatures from beyond the deep. Surely such magical wonders were at least as possible as finding a teenager whose greatest talent was the ability to be moulded by a music executive into next year's Big Thing.

———

"What makes you special?"

How would Holly answer, if someone asked her that? She was no longer sure.

CHAPTER TWO

MOONBEAMS IN A JAR MAY BE CLOSER THAN THEY APPEAR

Fake Geek Girl didn't break up, and they didn't break out. The band played their last gig down the Medea's Cauldron like normal on a Friday night, some time in January. They didn't come back the following week.

Holly, Sage and Juniper had all graduated, more or less. They'd aged out of the uni band demographic.

It wasn't like they meant to stop making music.

If anyone asked, in the three months that followed their last gig (which wasn't their last gig, not technically, because the band had definitely not broken up) they were working on their next album. For sure.

They'd put out two albums in three years. That was a hell of an achievement for a ragtag bunch of students with a solid but not astounding social media following. They'd had one viral hit, and they had a small, devoted fandom waiting for their next thing.

Fake Geek Girl was still here. Still alive. Still firing on all cylinders. Only...

Only, it was April.

Holly hadn't seen Juniper for ages. She'd barely seen Sage, and he lived in the flat upstairs so there was literally no excuse.

Life had sped up, somehow, from last year's comfortable slow roll of uni classes and casual jobs to, well. Whatever was happening now.

Mostly what was happening to Holly was Campion Merryweather.

Life as Campion's girlfriend (again, *still*) was fast and frantic. The sex was great, the conversation was tolerable, and every night meant another club, another happening. A secret concert, or an exclusive party. Holly had been here before, and it ended badly, but she knew better this time around. She wasn't invested in him. He was a placeholder, that was all. She could quit any time she liked.

Last year, when graduation started to loom over her, Holly found it was all a bit much. Decisions to be made, a future to build. She didn't know where to start.

Some shit went down on New Year's Day that sent shockwaves through her friend group. Nothing felt familiar any more; nothing felt safe.

So yeah, she had a weak moment, reconnected with her ex, and let him take the wheel.

Since then… well, there was a kind of peace in not making decisions for yourself. Even if that meant you forgot to keep in touch with your mates. Even if your sister moved out of the share house and you weren't 100% sure where she even lived now.

Even if you lost track of what exactly it was you'd thought you would be doing, after you left uni.

Week after week slid by, and Holly wasn't sure she was even in a band any more.

————

The job didn't help. Or rather, it helped a bit too well to fill the time and pay the rent and suck all her available energy out through a neon straw. "I can hook you up, babe, don't worry about it," drawled her boyfriend when Holly told him she wanted to make time for her music, after graduation.

Good old Campion. He was a fixer.

Somehow, 'making time for her music' translated into a casual job at MantiCore, Campion's dad's corporate music label, where Holly fetched coffees and drafted emails and never had a chance to think about song lyrics.

The money was decent — more than decent. And they didn't object to how she dressed like a ratbag muso, all ripped tights and technicolour hair. It was a good gig. She was lucky to have it.

But Holly couldn't even remember last time she even thought about writing a song.

———

This month, everything was all about Star Magic, the new reality TV show sponsored by MantiCore. Campion's own baby. As host and executive producer of the show, he fully expected this to be the thing that made him rich and famous beyond his dad's celebrity and money (even if, clearly, it required both those things to get off the ground).

Holly's 9-5 job quickly became a 9-9 job with working weekends. Apparently her main purpose in life now was to crush the spirit of tiny 'I want to be a star' hopefuls, and/or sweep up after them after they had their inevitable emotional meltdowns.

How was it April already?

———

Waiting at the bus stop on her way home, Holly dug out her battered lyrics notebook from the bottom of her lopsided messenger bag. Why did she even still carry this with her? What was she gonna write the next Fake Geek Girl song about?

Fetching coffee? The unbelievable banality of TV production behind the scenes? Cryptids?

The last entry in her notebook was December. Wild. Did she even exist if she wasn't writing songs?

(Did Fake Geek Girl exist, if they never saw each other? Were they a mythical creature, lost in the mists of time?)

Holly scrolled through her texts, wondering when she last talked to Juniper, and found their most recent exchange was weeks ago. Unacceptable.

Quickly, Holly typed:

> how many cryptid songs can you add to an album before it starts looking like that's the theme of the album?

There was no reply straight away, and Holly was distracted by having to snag the attention of the oncoming bus.

———

Later, after she collapsed on her couch hoping with all her heart that there were leftovers in the fridge to gnaw on, she saw there was a text from Juniper waiting for her.

> how many cryptids have broken your heart lately?

CHAPTER THREE
WOULDN'T EVERYONE RATHER BE A FISH?

"Sage!" Holly powered up the stairs into his kitchen and flung herself melodramatically at the table, scattering a pile of half-painted plastic orcs. "It's an emergency."

"What kind of emergency?" Her drummer leaned into the door frame, holding a steaming cup of coffee which smelled amazing. Sage was a big guy: broad shoulders, strong arms. Excellent hugger. Guaranteed to never wear a tie. He, at least, was a constant in her life.

"Talk to me about cryptids," she insisted. "I'm feeling inspired. Also, feed me. Mei's leftovers only go so far, and I am a starving musician."

"We're all starving musicians. You, Holly Hallow, are a scam artist." But Sage opened the fridge and pulled out a dish half-full of tuna casserole. "Lucky for you, Dec is out tonight chasing his new girl, and you can have his share."

"You're a prince among drummers," Holly assured him. "Heat it up instantly and I might not savage your leg."

Sage rolled his eyes, shoved the dish in the microwave and pushed some buttons. "Luckily for you I'm on my fourth coffee of the day, so I can do this without exploding the power grid."

"It's sweet you made that sacrifice for me," said Holly, deadpan. "It couldn't mean you're banging a high powered warlock and need to keep your power levels low to stay compatible? Blink twice if it's Jules again."

"It's too early in the morning to be interrogated by someone who's shagging Campion fucken Merryweather," said Sage.

"It's nighttime," Holly said pointedly. "Dark outside."

"It's too early in… the month. How's Hebes?"

"Haven't seen her."

"Me neither," said Sage glumly. "Sucks, right?"

"She'll be back. She's going through an independent phase." Holly didn't want to talk about her absent twin sister.

"Yeah?" Sage pulled the steaming casserole dish out of the microwave and set it down on the table, then produced two forks. As was usual with most of Dec's cooking, it was mostly protein and carbs, with the occasional pea rising to the surface. Salty. Cheesy. Delicious. "What phase are *you* going through right now, Hol?"

"Responsibility and pay cheques."

"Ugh."

"Tell me about it."

"What's all this about cryptids?"

"Okay." Holly tapped the side of the dish with her fork. "So we're making this stupid brainless TV show where we convince people we're going to find pop stars, but so far it's mostly queuing."

"Sounds about right for MantiCore."

"I want to write a song about how hunting for celebrity status is like searching for cryptids in like, banks and post offices."

"Do people still go into banks and post offices?"

"Maybe they don't. Maybe that's why the cryptids hang out there."

"Cryptids, they're like… mythical creatures, yeah?"

Holly nodded. "Bunyips and unicorns. Things that don't exist, but people think they do."

"I'm pretty sure unicorns exist. I dated a guy once who swore he was like, 25% unicorn."

"Magical creatures that are so good at hiding, they might as well not exist."

"But ice trolls are real. Goblins. Dryads. And, you know." Sage pointed at Holly, then at himself. "Witches are real."

"Yeti aren't."

"I once knew a bloke who claimed he tongue-kissed a yeti in a leather club."

"Did he document it with the World Cryptid Authority? No, he did not. Because it was bullshit, Sage."

"Kraken, though," he said thoughtfully.

"Okay, yes," Holly conceded. "I remember the news footage. Kraken are probably real."

"The Belladonna U Lake Beast."

"A mysterious singing ghost creature with tentacles, haunting the lower quad? Lies made up to terrify first years. That's barely even a lake, anyway. It's a puddle. Might as well call it the Belladonna U puddle beast."

"Drop bears."

"I'm not a tourist," Holly said sternly. "The important thing is…"

"The important thing," said Sage with his mouth full of fish and pasta, "is why are you telling me about your song instead of, you know, writing a song?"

Holly frowned. "I guess I was checking in that we still have a band. I haven't seen Juniper in weeks…"

"Juniper's in Tasmania."

She startled back. "What? No. Since when? *Why?*"

"Uh, her family are there."

"Her terrible family. In Tasmania. A mythical island probably full of drop bears. It can't be safe."

"She comes from… I mean, we all graduated, Hol."

"You're still at uni."

"Nah, I'm a postgrad, I only have to turn up once a week."

She scowled at him. "What's your point?"

"I mean, Juniper never lived here. She comes from Tassie, she roomed in dorms. Where did you think she would go when she graduated?"

This was the worst thing that anyone had ever said in Holly's presence. "She went *home*?"

"She went home," Sage confirmed.

"But we have to find her, bring her back. She's a third of the band, Sage!" How was he not utterly devastated? Why had no one told her?

Sage looked at her, steady, sympathetic. "And we definitely still have a band."

"*Yes*," said Holly. "I am writing a new song as we speak. An album. I'll write five albums if that means we get Juniper back."

Panic sparked inspiration, right? It had to. She could taste nothing but panic on the back of her tongue. Panic, and tinned tuna.

Juniper couldn't have *left* without saying goodbye.

"Well then," said Sage, still annoyingly chill about the disaster that had befallen them. "Stop wasting your time hunting cryptids, and start hunting mild-mannered Tasmanian cello players."

"Name?"

"Bella Moonchild Horizon."

"Do you have any equipment or magical needs we should be aware of?"

"When I sing, butterflies appear in the air."

"Good to know. What makes you special?"

"I know everyone probably says this, but... I just know I'm going to be a star."

———

I can't decide, if the song is about unicorns auditioning to be the one unicorn who saves the world, or if it's about unicorns holding auditions for like, the one human they're going to allow to survive the apocalypse.

After Holly sent the text, there was a long, agonising pause of at least eight minutes, in which two more prospective contestants of Star Magic explained exactly how they were it, the real thing, deserving of fame and fortune as the world's next Pop Sensation.

Finally, Juniper texted back:

why not both? You have a whole album to fill.

OMG the songs can't all be about unicorns, Junie

I can see the cover art now. Reckon we can get Sage to wear a rainbow horn?

Holly considered this very real possibility.

Worth a try.

———

"Name?"

"Tal Springer."

"Do you have any equipment or magical needs we should be aware of?"

"I hardly blow up microphones at all any more, but I do need a double shot caramel macchiato ten minutes before every performance. Preferably delivered by a hot girl."

"What makes you special? Apart from your dazzling charm."

"Isn't it obvious, luv? I'm gonna be a star."

———

R you rlly in Tasmania?

Holly texted, during her ten minute lunch break.

How did I not know that?

you were busy

Juniper texted back. Somehow, even in a basic text with no capitalisation, she managed to sound her usual low-key self. No accusing tone. No passive-aggressive layers. Or was it just in Holly's head, that the text sounded comforting, kind?

Letters on a screen. Tone was subjective. What did it mean that Holly looked at texts from Juniper, and felt warm all over?

> come home come home come home
> come home

she texted, in case it wasn't clear to Juniper that she was needed here.

> we have an album to record

A whole three minutes later, Juniper texted:

> write the songs first

Dots appeared after that, and vanished. Appeared, and vanished. Holly stared at them until her break was over, and it was time to return to work.

Another text came in, but it was from Campion and started with:

> Babe.

Holly could read it later.

———

"Name?"

"I call myself Sofia." A quiet voice: gentle. Barely there.

"Do you have any equipment or magical needs we should be aware of?"

"I don't think so. I'm only starting to understand my magic, but it doesn't seem harmful to humans."

"What makes you special?"

"I'm the Belladonna U Lake Beast."

Holly blinked. She stared at her notes, then up at the contestant. "I'm sorry?"

"I'm a lake beast," said the girl.

"You look like a person."

"Thank you."

She did, indeed look like a person. Sort of... a dull-looking person, really. Slightly pretty in an ordinary white girl way. Pale skin, soft brown hair that fell in barely-brushed ringlets to her shoulders. Basic clothes, cheap and practical. She looked like any other student, except that most of the teen girls auditioning today had made an effort, and this one was dressed like she was barely ready to leave the house.

"Lake beast," Holly repeated. "You mean — the mythical creature who haunts the lower quad, and sings at night. The one that Belladonna U students have been swapping weird stories about for more than a century. The one that is either dead, or doesn't exist, or both."

"Yes," said the girl, lifting her chin with confidence.

"You live in a *lake*?"

"I used to live in the lake. Some people found me, a few months ago. Now I live at their house."

Aw, share house hijinks. Holly remembered when that sort of thing happened to her.

"Aren't you supposed to have like, murderous sucking tentacles?"

The girl blushed, which at least brought a splash of colour to her cheeks. "I mean, you can't see them when I'm wearing clothes. And I haven't murdered anyone in decades."

Older than she looked, then. Quite the advantage for showbiz.

"But you sing?" Holly blurted out. This wasn't her question to ask. This early in the audition process, they had to figure out which candidates were worth putting on camera at all. Later on, that was when they started separating the genuinely great from the moderately good and the hilariously bad. (Only the great and the bad singers would be in the final cuts; Star Magic and Manti-Core had no time for moderate talent.)

The girl — Sofia — the Belladonna U Lake Beast — opened her mouth, and a glorious, terrible sound came out of it. Holly felt her whole body tighten in response, like she was being kissed and falling off a broom and hearing applause and setting off a magical fire alarm, all at the same time. She wanted to dance. She wanted to cry. She wanted to hug Juniper, right the hell now.

She wanted to know if her sister was okay.

"That's pretty good," she managed, her voice trembling. "I'll put you down as a maybe. Don't call us, we'll call you."

I found a cryptid

is that better or worse than finding a star?

I don't even know any more. Nothing makes sense.

Dots appeared, and disappeared, and appeared again. Holly waited, but Juniper had nothing else to say.

why aren't you here?

she typed, then deleted the words. Retyped them. Deleted them. *Take that. Stare at my dots for a change.*

CHAPTER FIVE

YOU CAN FLY ME TO THE MOON BUT YOU CAN'T MAKE ME DRINK

It was a cool club. That went without saying. Campion Merryweather only thrived amongst the fashionable, the edgy, the successful. Tonight, he was hosting a group of the more telegenic contestants of the show, to celebrate the first episode of Star Magic going to air.

Cosmic used to be a bookshop, Holly was pretty sure. Her sister Hebe had a part-time job here once. Now, the old brick building looked half-wrecked, a week or two away from being demolished. The walls were smeared with graffiti, half the floor was missing, and the remnants of fallen shelving still clung here and there, as if to remind you of what used to be.

Perfect venue for a pop-up club. One night only. Vodka cock-tails in bright plastic bottles, and a constellation magically cast upon the ceiling to make it look like they were partying on the surface of some abandoned asteroid.

The crowd were serenaded by a famous pop singer brought in from Bolivia, who was so underground she didn't even have social media accounts. She sang in a husky voice that created small bobbing lights with every note. The air around her sparked with barely-contained magic.

"That'll be you in a few months," crooned Campion, his arm

slung around Sofia the Lake Beast. "You're gonna be a star, baby."

The other contestants gave him dirty looks, like they hadn't expected him to be so obvious about picking favourites.

Holly, who as his girlfriend had seen this coming a mile off, rolled her eyes and got on with her job: tweeting photos of the contestants and the venue and the sultry, magical performer in the corner. Hashtag: #starmagicniteout

Yes, clubbing was her job now. Yay. Fun. One more thing to have the joy sucked out of it.

Sofia smiled shyly. A tentacle crept out of the sleeve of her jacket (Holly recognised the designer, one of Campion's favourites to buy for girls he planned to sleep with) and caressed his hand. "I bet you say that to everyone," she murmured.

Holly looked away, and took more pictures with her phone.

———

Later, she escaped the crowd and the sulky contestants, and the cryptid who was flirting with her boyfriend. There was no quiet spot, so she took a risk and went all the way out into the alley, knowing she might not get in again without Campion on her arm.

She tried to connect a call, but her phone was dead — too much magic swirling around in the club. It didn't look damaged, but the battery had been sucked dry. Holly rummaged in her tiny Eva Gorgon bag and pulled out a compact mirror, summoning one of the few MirrorWeb connections she knew by heart.

Juniper appeared, rumpled in pyjamas. "Holly? What's wrong?"

"I hate my job," Holly blurted out. "And my boyfriend. And my life, basically. What are you doing? Are you reading a book and drinking cocoa?" That sounded nice. Holly should do that. Why was she the sister who was terrible at domestic things?

"I was asleep," Juniper said. Even grouchy and exhausted,

there was a sweetness to her voice. "Because it's four in the morning."

Oh. "Fuck. Sorry."

"Also, my mum's sick."

Holly blinked rapidly. How many vodka satellites had she drunk? "Wait, what?"

Juniper sighed. "That's why I came back to Tasmania. My mum's sick. Nothing serious, but she needed me to look after her for a while. I thought it would be like, a week. That's why I didn't say goodbye or make a big deal of it. But... I don't have anywhere to live in the city yet, and it was just sort of easier to stay here until I figured things out. I want you to know, though. I didn't mean to *leave* leave. I just left. I'm coming back."

"When?" Holly begged. "I mean, um, Sorry about your mum. How's she doing?"

Juniper gave a brave, slightly wavering smile. "She's fine. She's starting to line up like, local orchestral auditions for me, so I need to get out of here soon. It's all good, Holly. Just a few more weeks."

For some reason that Holly couldn't understand at all, she felt like bursting into tears. "You promise?"

Juniper sighed, and she didn't look grouchy any more. "Hol. Your job, your boyfriend, your *life*. These are fixable things, you know. Go home. Drink some water. Write a song."

Her face flickered in the mirror, and then vanished.

Holly took a cab home. She didn't tell Campion where she was going.

Anyway, he never texted to ask.

In the morning, even before she got out of bed, Holly yanked over her messenger bag and scrabbled through it for the notebook, the one she'd been writing in again for a whole month now. Quickly, laboriously, she typed out all of the lyrics she had been working on. She hadn't even shown them to Sage yet. The song was entirely undercooked.

————

Am I invisible
      Or this this just what the future looks like
      I'm a voice in the walls
      I'm an hourly rate
      I think I forgot
      How I got in this state

But I remember being outrageous
      Don't you remember when we were
outrageous?
      We fought mythical beasts
      We shouted on stage
      We played beautiful music
      We were thunder and rage

      (too corny, stop rhyming, you're no good at it)

We were grit and lightning on a Saturday night

I forgot how to be a freaking unicorn
      Show me how
      I know you remember
      Show me now

We're all cryptids together, we're myth and we're
magic
      Everyone's special
      And that's my tragic

      (back story?)

———

Without thinking too hard, Holly booted up her recharged phone and texted the lyrics one line at a time to Juniper. A few minutes after she was done, those bloody dots appeared and then vanished.

> it's not a song yet

I know

That's the point.

You're supposed to help me finish it. Make it better.

> Is that my role in all this?

Holly typed and then deleted:

you make everything better

What she sent was:

hey Juniper, wanna be in a band? I kno a good one looking for a cellist. We gonna make you a star

> Seems fake

> Can't, sorry. Too loyal to my old band.

> They're going to get their act together any day now.

CHAPTER SIX
IN OTHER WORDS

"I rented the room," said Mei, two weeks later.

"Wait," said Holly, in the middle of scarfing down a bowl of Weet-Bix before she flew to work. "Hebe's room?"

"Hebe doesn't live here any more. We need to make rent."

"But," said Holly, blinking. "Hebe's room."

"I think you'll like the new housemate."

"Fine," muttered Holly, a bit hurt that this had all happened without her. Was Mei the organised one, now that Hebe wasn't around to make everything happen smoothly? Who voted on that? Maybe Holly could be the organised one, if anyone gave her half a chance. "Whatever, weirdo."

"Aren't you going to ask?" Mei called after her, as Holly stomped out of the house.

"I don't care!" Holly yelled back.

———

It was a shit day. Big Daddy Merryweather was in the studio, unsettling everyone with his Executive Energy. (If Campion was the Executive Producer, then his dad was Executive Executive, the God of Guess Who Put Up The Money.)

Holly was rattled, frazzled, frayed at the edges. The whole crew were jumpy. Even Sofia the Belladonna U Lake Beast only sang to half her usual disturbing ability, her tentacles limp and her eyes nervous. The director was pissed off. Half the tape was unusable.

Holly was yelled at by three different show contestants, all convinced that their star quality meant that the show was all about them.

"You should quit," said Campion, leaning over her desk at lunch time.

She stared at him. "What?"

"You should quit," he said sharply. "You only got this job because you were my girlfriend. I have someone else in mind for the position."

She had dumped Campion by text, the morning after that night at Cosmic. He never replied. Somehow she had imagined that maybe he wouldn't be a complete shit about it. But here they were.

Red fury stabbed behind Holly's eyes. Her magic tingled under her skin. On the far side of the studio, a power board sparked and the lights flickered. Campion Merryweather stepped back, looking slightly uncertain.

"You're a dick," said Holly, getting her her feet. "But also, I hate this job. So yes, I quit. Good idea. Best you've ever had."

She went by HR on her way out, and made a full report on the terrible working conditions at MantiCore.

Later, on the train home, she called her sister. Just to check in, see what she was up to. Hebe sounded genuinely pleased to hear her voice. So that was nice.

———

When Holly let herself into the downstairs flat, wrung out and jubilant but also somehow on the verge of tears, she found Juniper on her couch.

Warm, curvy Juniper, wearing a long lace skirt and a t-shirt covered in musical notation, her light brown hair tied up in a fancy knot with a clip like she had just walked off the set of a Jane Austen costume drama. She was writing in her diary with a pen that wrote in purple ink, and balancing a mug of tea on her knee.

Holly stared at her. *I'm in love with you,* she thought, stupidly. *When did that happen?*

What she said was: "You're home. About time."

"Yes," said Juniper, her face breaking into the loveliest of smiles. "Also, I live here now. Mei said it's okay for me to have Hebe's old room."

"You can have everything," Holly blurted out. "Um. It's good to see you. I quit my job."

Juniper looked startled. She shuffled her diary and mug to the coffee table, and stood up to enfold Holly in what had to be one of the all time top 3 hugs in recorded history. "Are you okay? What happened?"

"I got lost," Holly mumbled into her shoulder. "Also, I finally talked to Hebe and she sent me a spreadsheet of like, all the things I need to know to book local gigs for Fake Geek Girl. I want us to be a band again. For real."

"Makes sense," said Juniper. "I think you'll be great at managing us."

Relief washed over Holly. She had assumed she was having some kind of breakdown, but if it sounded logical to Juniper, it must be okay. "I'll need a job, obviously," she said. "Something that's not actively trying to destroy music. I can see if Cirque de Cacao is hiring."

"It's okay," Juniper said, patting her back. "You don't have to work everything out right this minute."

"I'm not a mess," said Holly. "I can get it together." It was important to her that Juniper know that.

"No one thinks you're a mess," Juniper said, giving her a stern look. "I believe in you, Holly Hallow. I always have."

"And I don't want to — it's not about being a star," Holly went on. There was a word ruined for her forever. "About being famous and all that shit. I just want to make music with you and Sage, and be *us*."

"I mean," said Juniper, her mouth twitching a little. "Getting famous is probably not the worst business plan in the world. But let's work on a new album, and see where we go from there."

Holly pulled her songwriting book out of her bag. "They're not all about cryptids," she said firmly. "Or unicorns, or celebrity, or freaking lake beasts. But I think… they're good. Getting there. Sage has been working on a few things too. If there's a theme, it's about — well. Growing up, figuring things out. I think."

"Sounds relatable," said Juniper, calm and sensible as ever. Reassuring. Wonderful. *Here*. "I love it. Let's get started."

THE YEAR OF CRITICAL
ROLLS

CHAPTER ONE
THE YEAR OF VIOLA
PART I

JANUARY.

- Recovery from all the New Year's drama.
- Thesis meetings.
- Unexpected travel grant.
- More meetings.

———

FEBRUARY

- Paris, apparently.
- The Academie des Sorcières, to be exact.
- Another tiny dorm room.
- More thesis to be written.
- But, in Paris.

———

MARCH

- More Paris.
- Occasional text from Jules, who has exactly nothing to say about his new job. (Suspicious)
- Radio silence from Chauv.

APRIL

- Paris in spring time. 9/10 would recommend.
- Long hours thesis writing indoors, total waste of Paris in spring time.
- Croissants.
- Wine.
- Cheese.

MAY

- Very important conference. Networking potential. Publishing opportunities.
- Why are all French professors so good-looking?
- All the wine.
- All the croissants.
- Thesis, what thesis?

(There's a court case beginning, back in Australia, but I don't think about it too hard. I recorded my testimony and sent it in on time. I've texted Chauv and Jules, but neither of them want to

talk about it either. Sure, some family friends tried to steal my magic, but how is that relevant to my thesis?)

- Croissants.
- Croissants.
- Wine.

_____

JUNE

Home.

Reality.

(Jules, you'd better pick me up from the airport, or the pornographic French novel I bought you about warlocks in love is going right in the rubbish bin.)

_____

It was something of a wrench for Viola Vale to discover that the distance between Paris in June at the beginning of a sun-drenched summer, and Melbourne in June at the beginning of a very grey winter was exactly one long-haul plane flight.

Air travel was hard on a witch. Flying by broomstick made sense at a visceral level; it made you feel at one with the magical universe. Strong, and connected to the sky.

A metal box with wings stood against everything that nature had to offer. You were ripped away from the earth and insulated from the air. Why had no one used magic to develop portals yet? Step into a cauldron in Paris, step out of a different cauldron in

Australia... and, of course, if you hated it there, you could nip back for a croissant any time you liked.

Viola was a little bit in love with Paris.

Still, it wasn't the weather that made her dread coming home, or the sub-standard pastries, or the fact that she'd barely spoken to her friends in months.

No, it was the familiar clang of a deadline that made her feel hollow inside. Six months. She had six months left to complete her doctoral thesis. She'd promised herself she'd do so much reading on the plane, and instead she found herself caught in a loop of Season 1 of *The Bromancers*, a show that usually irritated her beyond all belief.

If the choice was between finishing her thesis or getting way more into *The Bromancers* than a normal person ever should, then bring on the unresolved sexual tension between handsome warlocks and their car. She was here for it.

To top it all off, Jules didn't pick her up. Another sign that Something Was Wrong. Picking you up from the airport was an essential BFF duty. Mind you, answering mirrorchat updates was also an essential BFF duty and Viola had been just as remiss in that over the last several weeks as her friends.

(*Paris*, she didn't want to spend half of Paris attached to a mirror... that was her excuse and she was sticking to it.)

At least Jules hadn't completely abandoned her. He sent a substitute to pick her up from baggage claim. He sent Sage McClaren.

Viola saw him before he saw her, standing head and shoulders above the world's tiniest family of aunties, who all had giant signs for a returning niece. Sage was blessedly sign-free. He wore a Kraken t-shirt that she was sure she had stolen from him a year ago, another alarming sign.

The universe was awry. Nothing would be quite be right again… until she submitted her thesis.

"Why aren't you Jules?" she demanded as soon as she stepped off the escalator.

"Nice to see you too, Vale. C'mon, don't want to miss the spinny thing with the suitcases. Best bit of air travel."

He cut a path through the clusters of tourists and locals, just by walking while owning those shoulders. Annoyed that she had to trot after him, Viola did her best to be dignified while keeping up. Damn her short legs.

"What happened to Jules?" she tried, but talking to his back was almost as pointless as talking to his face.

"Don't worry about it. What does your suitcase look like?"

"Expensive," she snapped. "Why are you here, Sage?"

He glanced over his shoulder, and disarmed her with the widest, warmest smile available. That smile was like being hugged by a celebrity in a cardigan. "We're mates, aren't we? It's what you do for a mate who's been poshing it up in France for the best part of the year."

"I didn't bring you a present," she grumbled.

"Your presence is present enough," he said with the smirk of a bloke who knew full well that she had in fact brought him a present.

(It was a stupid enamel pin that said *C'est une rock star*, she had got two of them, one for him and one for Holly. Juniper got one that said *Ou est le biblioteque* because Viola thought she was more of a book person than a rock star person, and there were no cute French pins that referenced cellos. Damn it, she hated that she had a suitcase full of thoughtful baubles for people she didn't even like.)

The next ten minutes was a blur of waiting and staring at suitcases, wondering if her own would ever appear through the little hatch.

There was a troupe of Bulgarian wizards blocking every exit, all of them irritable as their caffeine pills (essential to block strong magic from interfering with flight controls) began to wear off.

Then there was the car park. Just, so much car park.

"So," Viola said tiredly as she finally climbed into the front seat of Sage's battered van. "What's so vital that Jules bloody Nightshade can't roll out of bed at 6pm to pick up his best friend from the airport?"

"It's a secret," said Sage, looking slightly hunted.

Viola groaned. "It's not… there's not some kind of bullshit surprise party waiting at the house, is there? I've just been in the air for more than a day, I am not up for a comedy French-themed party with baguettes and strings of onions."

She had agreed, reluctantly, to take up the offer of crashing at the Manic Pixie Dream House for a couple of nights, because her old dorm room wasn't available until after the weekend. Some random exchange student had been staying there for the last several months, because Belladonna U never missed the opportunity to make a buck.

She was too old to be living in residential halls, but she couldn't face starting real life yet, not with that bloody thesis hanging over her head. Next year. She could be a grown up next year.

In Paris, Viola had thought, what harm would it do to spend a couple of days putting up with share house shenanigans? Now she wished she'd booked a hotel instead.

"Cross my heart," said Sage, driving his van through several complicated turns as he pulled them out of the labyrinthine car park and on to the highway. "No one's throwing you a party, Vale."

In retrospect she should have taken more note of the way he swallowed a laugh on the word 'party,' but she was already closing her eyes, too tired to care about his stupid private joke.

This was so much worse than she could have imagined.

Viola let her travel bag slide slowly off her shoulder, as Sage set her suitcase down in the corner.

At a large round table in the centre of Holly and Mei's downstairs living room, four faces turned to look at her. Mei. Dec. Jules. Juniper. The table was covered with dice and strange cardboard shapes that looked a lot like cakes.

Viola gave the four of them her most baleful glare. "No," she said.

"Vale!" Jules leaped up to hug her, and she was exhausted enough that she let him. "I missed you, darling. Sorry I couldn't collect you myself, things are crazy at work right now."

Work. She wasn't even sure what his job was. How was he a work person? Were suits involved? He was dressed in his usual very expensive shirt and trousers, but his hair was rumpled.

"I missed… something. Since when are you a gaming nerd? I've only been gone a few months!" Viola gave Sage a dirty look over Jules' shoulder, which she only half meant. "What did you do to him?"

"Domesticated him," said Sage, looking smug. "You're welcome."

"Are you going to play, Viola?" asked Juniper nicely. Damn it. Juniper was always nice.

"We can always use a Monster of the Week," agreed Mei in her usual deadpan voice. "That's not an insult. It's actually a high honour."

Viola sighed, and looked directly at Dec. Her ex. She'd known she would see him here — he lived upstairs, after all. But she hadn't been braced for impact when it came to warm brown eyes looking at her like he was pleased to see her, for entirely platonic reasons.

Later, she would blame it on the jet lag.

"Can I play without you explaining the stupid game to me?" she tried.

"Of course!" said Jules, yanking her into a chair. "I'll lend you my dice. Right. So it's based on this dessert-themed anime series called Cake Wizards..."

Viola hated it already. She was not prepared for Jules to have turned into someone who owned his own dice. But.

She'd missed home. And these ridiculous people. Everything about this year already felt so big, so important, so *everything hangs in the balance*. Half the people in this room had real jobs now. And yet, they still had time to hang out and play a stupid dice game. "Tell me there's actual cake, not just fictional made-up cake."

"You'll be playing a Torte Tornado," said Sage, sounding proud of himself. "No cake, but everyone brought Tim Tams. We have a ziggurat of Tim Tams."

Oh, well. Okay. As long as there were Tim Tams.

"Just this once," said Viola. "I mean it. I'm not going to make a habit of this."

They all looked delighted. She hated them all.

JANUARY

The first episode of Cake Wizards screens internationally, and becomes instantly popular with tweens, forty-something mums nostalgic for the cartoons of the 1980s, and university students.

Also, Mei. Mei really likes it. This will be important later.

———

FEBRUARY

"Sage."

"No."

"Sage!"

"No."

"You have to watch this. You're gonna love it. I want to run an RPG based on it. There's wizards and cake. It's only 40 episodes, you can do that in a weekend."

"Mei, I don't have time to fall in love with another freaking anime series."

"*Sage.*"

———

MEICAKES HAS CREATED THIS MIRRORCHAT.

Meicakes: Dec.

Dodecohedron: Seen it. Love it.

Meicakes: So you'll...

Dodecohedron: Yep.

Meicakes: Awesomecakes. [Dancing Cakemoji x 3]

———

MARCH

NIGHTSHADE HAS CREATED THIS MIRRORCHAT.

Nightshade: I don't understand

Meicakes: I know, its adorable

Nightshade: my character is supposed to be good at magic AND cake decorating. So wtf is happening

Meicakes: This is what you get for rolling a 1. It's a critical fail, nothing to be done. Disaster must ensue.

Nightshade: I DON'T FAIL AT THINGS, MEI

Meicakes: you know, sometimes even if you're a genius level cake decorator, someone accidentally throws an incendiary hex in the sprinkles jar and your whole mission is blown. Just like in real life.

Nightshade: so how do I roll better dice?

Meicakes: I mean, they were borrowed dice, not sure what you expected here

Nightshade: where do I buy good dice?

Meicakes: I like that you're taking this seriously. But this isn't necessarily a thing you can throw money at

Meicakes: who am I kidding, gaming is totally a thing you can throw money at, let me send you some links

———

MEICAKES HAS CREATED THIS MIRRORCHAT

Meicakes: So. No Hebe.

SagePlaysDrums: did she even message you?

Meicakes: oh yeah, there was like a Level 2 excuse.

Meicakes: do you know what's up with her?

SagePlaysDrums: Nah

SagePlaysDrums: it sucks

SagePlaysDrums: I miss her

Meicakes: she'll be back. No one can resist Cake Wizards forever

———

APRIL

MEICAKES HAS CREATED THIS MIRRORCHAT

Meicakes: It's OK you know

HebeHallow: [Question Mark Dancemoji]

Meicakes: you don't have to come up with a new excuse every fortnight.

HebeHallow: I was definitely going to come this week

Meicakes: you're always welcome

Meicakes: but, you know

Meicakes: we're not expecting you

HebeHallow: it's too late to join, isn't it? I know. I've missed too many sessions. I'm really sorry

Meicakes: never 2 late babe

HebeHallow: maybe later in the year when things settle down a bit. You know how it is. Life after uni.

Meicakes: [Icecream Sundae Dancemoji]

———

MAY

"So... Juniper. You're back."

"I am. I live here now. You're looking very serious, Mei. Is this a roommate review?"

"Noooo, we are all very casual and low stress and if there was a roommate review then you would absolutely be ten out of ten, would roommate again, but we don't do roommate reviews, so don't worry about it. But absolutely keep mopping the kitchen floor, I am very excited about how often you do that."

"I know it's a bit weird because... Hebe. You all lived together for so long. You and Holly have your routines."

"Yep yep yep."

"Mei, is there something you want to ask me?"

"It's just. Okay. The thing is. Doyouwannaplaycakewizardswithus?"

"Cake Wizards."

"Yes, it's an anime series."

"Are you kidding me? Of course I know what Cake Wizards is. I've been writing Lucifell and Lafayette fanfic for two months now."

"OMG."

"OMG. But you said play, is there a game? Are you... ARE YOU DOING A CAKE WIZARDS RPG?"

"YES, YES WE ARE."

"OMG."

"OMG. So you want to —"

"YES OBVIOUSLY. CAN I BE A CREME PAT PALADIN?"

———

JUNE

"The Torte Tornado is swaying back and forth, but still active."

"Howwww is it still alive?"

"Especially considering Vale has been asleep on me for the last ten minutes."

"Captain Fondant will be unconscious for another two turns. Cornetto is still wedged in the mousse of unusual size. Madrigal?"

"How far away are my gateaux knives?"

"They landed about half a kilometre away."

"Fuck. I guess I punch the giant dessert tornado with my bare hands, then."

"Nightshade, you're a spindly little sugar elf, this is not going to go well."

"Shush, Sage, he made his choice. Roll for combat."

"FUCK."

"Oh dear. There's Jules' critical fail for the evening, everyone take a drink. So Madrigal the sugar elf is swept up by the Torte Tornado and flung three kilometres away. Roll for luck…"

"Eleven."

"You land in a tree. You're alive. Dec, Elinor the Ginger-bread Witch is the only one left on her feet."

"I use one of my pre-set spells — Bun in the Oven."

"Oh, NICE. Roll for spell-casting."

"Fifteen, plus the bonus…"

"So that works. A piece of the tornado about the size and shape of Elinor's oven is transported to her cottage to be baked until burnt. The Torte Tornado is struggling to maintain its shape now, and four of its twelve eyes have fallen closed. It's in a bad way. Viola, can you roll a D20?"

"Yeah, she's definitely asleep on my shoulder."

"Someone roll Viola's D20?"

"4."

"The Torte Tornado explodes, splattering cake crumbs and custard over the county. Hallelujah, it's raining torte. That is combat done for this evening, and that's a wrap for us, because I have an early start tomorrow and I'm sick of all your beautiful faces."

"That was awesome, Mei."

"Great night."

"Come on, Vale. Wake up, sweetheart. Holly says you can sleep in her bed tonight."

"Oh, hmm. Where's Holly sleeping?"

"It's a mystery."

"Shut UP, Sage."

"Nightshade." (Yawn) "Is this Australia?"

"So I hear."

"Did I win your stupid game?"

"Uh… sure. You won. Then to celebrate, you leapt into the air and scattered yourself over a wide area."

"Nice."

JULY

"ONE."

"Drink!"

"This is is getting silly now. Okay, So Madrigal the sugar elf fails so catastrophically at flirting with the Sorbet Queen, you all get thrown out of the palace, and she refuses to reward you for your last quest."

"I swear, this is my third set of dice. Why does this keep happening?"

"Jules, you need to make a dice jail. Show those dice who's boss. That'll whip them into shape."

"Tell me more about… dice jail."

AUGUST

"Check for traps."

"I mean, it's a pit. You're all already trapped, in a giant pit. This is the trap."

"I use my all-seeing emerald to check for further traps within the trap."

"There are no traps here besides the pit you have all fallen into. As you look up, you see the glowing light of a forcefield spell over the top of the pit."

"Can I heal Captain Fondant?"

"Sure, but nothing happens for the next hour or so, and he'll have healed up by then anyway."

"What happens after the hour?"

"I'M SO GLAD YOU ASKED. An hour has passed. You're all well-rested, and a bit bored. Suddenly the pit fills with what can only be described as ominous theme music. Just a sec…"

(Ominous theme music fills the room)

"Nice touch."

"Thanks, Dec. You all look up, to see a sinister silhouette overhead. It is Aerie Berry, the dark queen of sponge."

"…"

"Oooh?"

"Yay?"

"IT IS AERIE BERRY, THE DARK QUEEN OF SPONGE."

"Oh, that's my cue? Here I am."

"Viola!"

"Were you hiding in the bedroom?"

"Mei wanted to make a grand reveal."

"Yes, it was all very grand. Why aren't you wearing the costume?"

"Mei, there is no world in which I would have worn the costume."

"Not even the hat?"

"Good to see you, Vi. Couldn't keep away?"

"Well, you know how much I love it when you all refer to me as Monster of the Week. So flattering. Wait. Where the hell is Jules?"

"Uh, something came up. Work thing?"

"*Work thing?*"

———

SEPTEMBER

"And the cave opens up in front of your party to reveal… a cupcake tower, a three headed dog, and…"

"MEDUSA, THE SNAKE-HEADED GORGON."

"Nice one, Vi. Still no wig?"

"Fuck off, Dec."

OCTOBER

MEICAKES HAS CREATED THIS MIRRORCHAT

Meicakes: No Jules again, so Madrigal the Sugar Elf continues his spiritual side quest. Viola's continuing her role as Medusa this month... unless you're ready for a proper player character, V?

Violacakes: no

Dodecohedron: we'll get you in the end, Vi

Meicakes: Sage, we need to have a private chat about Captain Fondant's secret shit

SagePlaysDrums: [Thumbs up Dancemoji]

Meicakes: any other notes for our next few sessions?

Violacakes: ELVISH [Headdesk Dancemojis x 3]

Meicakes: is this a game thing or IRL thing?

Violacakes: it's a my thesis needs to die thing. Apparently I have to learn enough Elvish in the next 2 weeks to read a bunch of papers I know aren't going to be remotely helpful to my argument, just to prove I read them.

SagePlaysDrums: that happened to me with my Honours thesis only it was two months ago and it was one book in Deep Gnomeon that literally no one knows how to translate.

Violacakes: so not the same at all then

Meicakes: I had an ex who used to speak Elvish. I guess they probably still do

Violacakes: DO YOU HAVE THEIR NUMBER?

———

NOVEMBER

"Well, look who it is. The amazing disappearing sugar elf."

"Mei! Where is everyone?"

"If you'd been following our group mirrorchat, you'd know they all ditched this week. Except Juniper, of course, who just headed out with Holly to buy me consolation pizza."

"I'm sorry. I know I've been a dick."

"It's not cool to ghost the DM, Nightshade. Are you okay? You look wrecked."

"Cheers, thanks a lot."

"Sit down before you fall down. Tea? Booze? Cream of vervain for dreamless sleep?"

"Can I just hang out here for a bit?"

"I'm texting Juniper now to get an extra pizza."

"Not hungry, just… gonna lie down here on the couch for a minute."

———

"Is that Jules asleep on our couch, or do we have to help you hide a body?"

"The first one."

"Good, wouldn't want the pizza to get cold."

———

"Ugh."

"Welcome back to the land of the living, Nightshade. We saved you half a pizza because we're excellent friends."

"What is that on the TV? With all the pink and the… cupcake battles?"

"It's Cake Wizards, obvs."

"Cake Wizards is a show?"

"Oh, you sweet summer child."

———

DECEMBER

"Welcome to the final Cake Wizards gaming session of the year! In which we have a full house."

"Wooo!"

"Thanks for turning up, you arses."

"We love you, Mei."

"It's been a glorious campaign, with remarkably few player deaths, despite Jules' amazing ability to critical fail under pressure, and we are so close to Lamington Mountain, I can taste it. We now have three hours — everyone put all mirrors and phones away — to complete this final quest arc, rescue the Sherbet Prince from the Lollipop Guild, and win your hearts' desires. Got it?"

"Yes, Mei."

"Can I just text —"

"NO."

"Don't have to all yell at once."

"That was actually just Mei."

"Before we begin, Viola couldn't make it tonight…"

"Boo!"

"Because she's doing the final crossing the T's, dotting the I's of her fucking thesis this weekend, but I do have a special guest to introduce to you all. When we left off, Madrigal, Elinor,

Captain Fondant and Cornetto were all hanging off a dangling rope bridge over the edge of the Lemon Squash Ravine. Cornetto spotted a mysterious hand in a sparkly glove taking hold of the rope. As you all look upwards, you see a matching pink sparkly pointed hat and robes, and a very familiar face from your days at Cake University. It's…"

"PROFESSOR PLUMCAKE!"

"Hebe!"

"OMG."

"You wore the costume. *She wore the costume.*"

"Is that hand-beading?"

"Heebs."

"Sage. Everyone. I know I've been kind of apart from everything this year, but I just want to say —"

"Hebe, shut up and sit down. We all appreciate the homemade costume but we have less than 3 hours to get this done. If you have to say anything, say it as Professor Plumcake."

"Professor Plumcake loves you all so much."

"We love you too, Heebs."

"And…"

"Oh, yes, sorry Mei. I forgot. Smiling and blowing kisses at you all, your old mentor Professor Plumcake draws a shiny sword and cuts the rope."

"WHAT."

"WTF."

"You will all hit the water in six seconds. Roll for initiative. You too, Hebe."

"4"

"17"

"6"

"12"

"13"

"Jules goes first."

"Can I use that magic egg I got from the ganache goblins?"

"Roll a D20 and we'll find out."

"Oh here we go."

"Why is everyone laughing?"

"Because Jules Nightshade has rolled more ones than any newbie player ever. One time, his character was trying to do a rabbit out of the hat trick to entertain a small child in a tavern, and the rabbit exploded."

"I hate you all."

"..."

(Wild screaming and laughter)

"A 20 is good, right?"

"Yes, Jules. It's very good. I know you've never had a good dice roll before, but it means nice things happen to your characters. In this case, the magical egg soars out of your pocket and breaks open, spilling forth a green gas that forms into a friendly, obliging dragon."

"Excellent. Hold on to your hat, Professor Plumcake. As soon as we all climb the hell on to the back of this dragon, Madrigal the sugar elf will be your doom."

JANUARY

The office is grey. Various shades of grey as if it is trying to project 'normality' as hard as possible.

Jules is wearing blue. A bright, glittering suit of cerulean which seemed like a fabulous idea in the shop when he was deliberating job interview apparel.

Vale was not there to stop him picking cerulean. She's not here now. No hand-holding for you, young Nightshade.

No coffee, either. His magic is about ready to vibrate him all the way through the thick grey floor.

Three warlocks enter: two male-presenting, one female. All in grey suits. All with flat, unfriendly faces.

A job interview or an interrogation? It's starting to sink into Jules that he was on the verge of being arrested really quite recently, and these people probably know all the details.

"Mr Nightshade," says the woman. "Your application was impressive." She says this in the same tone she might say "I hear you murdered seven puppies."

Well, if they're going to be like that, there's no point in

holding back. Might as well give them the full Nightshade treatment.

Jules tips back his head, rolls up his mouth in a superior snarl. "I didn't apply for this job."

The problem with being the grandson of a powerful warlock with business interests across the country is that job offers proliferate like weeds, usually with some kind of dodgy corporate catch to them.

(The other problem is of course that your ordinary person friends can't be remotely sympathetic to you about something so outrageously privileged as strings being pulled for your 'benefit' constantly and without your consent, and even if you say such things aloud you sound like such a whiny brat you end up despising yourself.)

She smiles, briefly; an unpleasant turn of events. "All the more impressive. You come highly recommended. And we think you're exactly what we need."

Jules sighs. "I know who you are and what you can do. That means you know exactly what offers I've had for work since graduation, and what kind of financial packages are in consideration. Why exactly should I give all that up to work for this drab little government outfit?"

All three of the grey warlocks look intrigued. That wasn't the result he was hoping for.

"We believe you're a good person," says one of them.

"Oh fuck," says Jules, surprised into laughter. "You really do need help."

FEBRUARY

Jules has supper with Mother at the Morgana Hotel once a week. His grandfather owns it; a junior management position was among his graduation offers. Jules could not imagine a worse starter job than trying to convince old Julius he's worthy of inheriting the Nightshade empire one day.

(If he is going to impress the old man, better to do so from a distance.)

Supper is always delightful, delectable, first class.

(He usually needs to grab some real food afterwards.)

Mother is in an odd mood. She pushes her braised spinach around and around the salmon-chard drizzle. Maybe it's her disappointment in her son. Maybe it's her court case against people who used to be her best friends. Maybe she also is craving a dirty cheeseburger with extra onion and a fried egg.

"I'm not disappointed," she says, finally.

"You are."

"Just — if you're going to do that kind of work, darling, the least you could do is let me brag about it at the club. It's so *worthy*."

"No can do. Tell them I'm doing something in the city."

"I can't be more specific?"

"Your friends won't care. I'll drift by your book club every few months in a designer suit, and they will not ask further questions. Guaranteed."

"I suppose that means you want me to enlarge your clothing allowance, darling."

"Well, I won't be paying for it out of my government salary."

They laugh; hers is a little bitter, but she still calls for the dessert menu.

"Fine. We're celebrating."

"Oh," says Jules. "Is that what we are?"

———

MARCH

Serenity Jones is an angry woman. A tiny, fierce ball of impatience, sarcasm, and sharp, sudden movements.

"You can't have a life," she said to Jules on the first day he was assigned to her as partner. "Friends, lover, family. This job will make them all hate you. You might as well get used to being alone."

"That's okay," drawled Jules. "My friends already hate me."

Her magic is the opposite of her personality. It's a cool drink of water on a sunny day. There's a warmth to it, but it doesn't clash against his power like Sage's; like Viola's. Sharing a space with Serenity Jones is like having half an espresso shot in his bloodstream. He's never felt so centred.

Serenity Jones is ten years older than Jules Nightshade, and she treats him like a toddler who has barely learned to walk.

———

He likes the work. *Real Intelligence.* Jules as always enjoys situations that make him feel smarter than anyone else. He likes walking into the office alongside the compact fury of Serenity Jones.

He loves fieldwork. They don't do much yet — he's a baby trainee, their missions are minor. Mostly it involves sitting in cafes or bars, quietly absorbing the magical signature of People of Interest.

Occasionally, they get to Make a Scene, which means going into some abandoned safe house, hotel room or Air B&B, and soaking up every hint of magical resonance left behind. Then, writing complex and lengthy reports about every stray hex he sucked out of the carpet.

It's drudge work, according to Jones.

Jules is having a great time.

Most of all, he likes the fact that, six weeks into their partnership, Serenity Jones doesn't seem to think he's a total waste of space. She's started sharing stories — big missions, international diplomacy, hilarious anecdotes, mostly about how much she hates every co-worker she's ever had.

Being tolerated by Serenity Jones is like being adored by anyone else. He'll take it.

Isolating himself from other people though? Fuck that. How's that worked out for his mother over the years, hiding in her family hotel like she's a princess in the tower? How's that worked out for Chauv, who won't answer calls any more? Or Vale, who left the actual shitting country to get away from them all?

Jules respects Serenity Jones. He does not want to become her.

———

NIGHTSHADE HAS CREATED THIS MIRRORCHAT.

Nightshade: Can I ask a favour?

Meicakes: New mirror, who dis?

Nightshade: Hilarious

Meicakes: Are we even linked? You've never messaged me on here before.

Nightshade: It's about Wizard Cakes

Meicakes: HOW DARE U

Meicakes: It's Cake Wizards

Nightshade: That's what I said

Meicakes: ...

Nightshade: I want in on your new game.

Meicakes: why

Nightshade: I've discovered a deep inner obsession with wizards who are also cakes, and I need to act that out by some kind of performative dice-based group gaming activity.

Meicakes: seems fake

Meicakes: wait, is this part of an elaborate plan to get back with Sage?

Nightshade: no, it's an elaborate plan to avoid becoming isolated from real life now I have a job that requires more of me than I ever thought possible [MESSAGE NOT SENT]

Nightshade: yes?

Meicakes: so lucky I ship you two. First game's at 4pm Saturday. Bring snacks. You will be required to cosplay as your character, so bring pointy ears, some nose putty and any clothing items made from silver mesh

Nightshade: I have been assured by a third party that cosplay is not compulsory, and I am allowed to resist any social pressure to look foolish

Meicakes: Sage will be wearing blue paint and very little else.

Nightshade: is there a preferred brand of nose putty?

APRIL

It's been months since Jules last saw Sage naked; it was worth the wait.

They almost tumbled back into bed back at New Year's, after that clusterfuck of a party turned into Chauvelin's family tragedy. Surely if anyone had earned 'glad my friend's house didn't kill us' sex, it was the two of them.

It didn't happen then. Months later, Jules finally takes matters into his own hands.

They've had their wild tumbles, their fiery arguments, their public gropings and intense, passionate hook ups.

Now, as it turns out…

Slow, comfortable "hey why don't you stay over so we can work on your character's backstory" sex is also pretty great.

"I have to get up early for work," Jules mumbles into Sage's shoulder. His large, warm, slightly sticky shoulder. Best shoulder.

"No worries," says Sage, half asleep. "Come back tomorrow night, yeah? We still have to figure out what secrets your character is keeping."

Ah yes. He's playing a secretive sugar elf. Nothing like real life at all.

———

MAY

Irene Nightshade successfully sues Nicholas and Mereen Chauvelin for endangering her son with their careless magical experiments.

(The criminal case will proceed later in the year, if it doesn't get postponed again.)

Irene Nightshade can now afford to buy a second hotel, should she wish to do so.

Jules has some feelings about this.

He doesn't share them with anyone.

And then it occurs to him that this is a terrible life choice.

Do better, Nightshade. Grow the fuck up.

———

NIGHTSHADE HAS CREATED THIS MIRRORCHAT.

Nightshade: are you avoiding me

Chauvelin: of course not

Chauvelin: I know you never had to make much of an effort at university, but this year is kind of killing me. So many essays. Unreal social studies is even tougher than political history.

Nightshade: so it's not about the parents thing then?

Chauvelin: ...

Chauvelin: don't be an arse

Nightshade: heard anything from Hebe lately? Weird she doesn't live here any more.

Chauvelin: here?

Chauvelin: are you at my house

Nightshade: game night, baby

Nightshade: you could join us. Roll some dice. Fight some giant gateaux monsters. Or you could play a giant gateaux monster, and we'd fight you

Chauvelin: no thanks

Nightshade: you know Vale's coming back next month. Any thoughts?

Nightshade: Chauv, thoughts?

Nightshade: fuck you, then

———

JUNE

"Seriously, Nightshade?"

"McClaren, I wouldn't ask if it wasn't important."

"Vale's going to murder you."

"Not as hard as she'd murder me if I stranded her at the airport."

"And you can't tell me why."

"It's work. You know how it is. If nothing serious comes up, I'll make the game by the skin of my teeth, but there's no way I can leave an hour early to meet an international flight."

"And you had no one else to ask?"

"Aren't you the person I *get* to ask?"

"…"

"I didn't mean that."

"Oh, I think you meant it."

"Stop fucking smirking."

"I'm your person."

"I didn't say that. You tricked me."

"*Mate.* I was just hinting you should admit why you're not asking Ferd. I wasn't looking to define the relationship."

"Chauvelin and I haven't exactly been talking."

"I know. That's what I was hinting. I'm not a complete bastard. Shut and kiss me, yeah?"

"All I said was — mmph."

"I know what you said."

———

JULY

- Work
- Sleep
- Cake Wizards
- Sage

———

AUGUST

MEICAKES HAS STARTED THIS MIRRORCHAT

Meicakes: I can't believe you missed it

Meicakes: Viola came back to play Monster of the Week

Meicakes: she was brutal

Meicakes: this is the second session you've missed, Jules

Nightshade: I know. Sorry.

———

SEPTEMBER

- Work
- Sleep
- Sage

OCTOBER

- Work
- Sleep

———

NOVEMBER

- Work

This month has been all about surveillance. Sitting in cars. Bars. Skanky flats overlooking dodgy warehouses. The works.

Jules is bored out of his skull.

"One more," drawls Serenity, her hand clawed around a can of Beltaine, one of those horrible herbal drinks that are so on-trend. Sugar and grass clippings. You might as well drink tea. "One more day and we'll be rotated back to paperwork for the rest of the year."

"Hail to the Kindly Ones," Jules sighs.

"You'll get your weekends back. Rock bands and biscuit orcs, whatever you kids are into these days."

He regrets telling her about Cake Wizards.

"How's that big-armed BF of yours?" she asks, angling into the corner of the window so she gets the best view without being seen from below.

"If I ever get a chance to see him, I'll find out if he's still talking to me."

"Didn't deny the BF label I see."

"I'm tired," he yawns. "I'll fight your heteronormative assumptions another time. What even is this job?"

"Dodgy passports."

"Really?" He laughs hollowly. "Bit of a come-down."

Last month, it was all about mobsters trying to export native animals for rich zillionaires overseas. Nightshade and Jones were a small part of a larger team, but they still got a commendation for it.

This month, dodgy passports.

"Could be bigger than it looks," says Serenity. "Our source says this guy has been supplying wealthy warlocks with new identities for years. And there's some kind of big fish rumoured to be making contact this week…"

Jules rolls his eyes, and makes them a cup of tea. He's never made so many cuppas in his life, before he took on this job. He's still a trainee. He knows his place.

"Could be something," murmurs Serenity, just as a swell of familiar magic rolls over them both. The presence of powerful warlocks who are too arrogant to hide themselves.

Jules' own magic spikes hard; prickles of ice form on the backs of his hands. "I know that magical signature," he whispers in a panic. "Serenity, *I can't be here.*"

———

DECEMBER

"I'm a spy," Jules says aloud, finally blurting the words he's been keeping hidden all year. "I work for the — it's not hex development, not private surveillance. I work for the government in Real Intelligence, I'm a fucking spy. And the pay is *shit.*"

The silence after his confession is awful, just for a moment. Jagged, and frozen.

Then Chauv and Vale begin to laugh at him.

CHAPTER FOUR
THE YEAR OF VIOLA
PART 2

JULY

- Back to reality. Tutoring. Dorm room. Thesis thesis thesis. Library library library.
- Footnotes.
- So many footnotes.
- Never leave the footnotes until this late in the process. Lesson to learn for... next time you do a doctoral thesis. You idiot.
- Coffee.
- Chocolate.
- No sleep.

———

AUGUST

Viola was thinking about Pandora. She was usually thinking about Pandora. The mythological figure at the heart of her thesis. The first mortal woman of Greek mythology. Protector of the jar. Guardian of the Real.

Viola was not expecting Medusa.

She tripped over her feet on the pavement, staring into a shop that was, apparently, mostly lamps and throw cushions.

Lamps, throw cushions and Medusa the snake-haired gorgon. A terracotta statue, glazed in turquoise. Surrounded by home furnishings, as part of a frankly spectacular window display.

Viola knew that statue. Not only because it used to sit in her ex-boyfriend's kitchen, but also because the face was her own.

Somehow, she couldn't take her eyes off Medusa, *off her own stony gaze*. So many questions.

Then a shop girl twitched a bone-white curtain aside to adjust some of the throw cushions and stared at Viola, caught in her gorgon gaze.

Hebe Hallow.

———

"You work here now?" Viola asked, once she made it inside the store. She didn't really have to ask the question. The whole place felt like Hebe's magic: warm and inviting. Like a cup of tea balancing perfectly on the curved arm of a comfortable chair.

"I do," said Hebe.

"Where are you living? I haven't seen you at the house since I've been back."

Not that Viola herself was there constantly — the thesis didn't allow her to have much of a social life. When it all got too much, though, when she was feeling lonely or frustrated or sick of the sight of the footnotes, she'd walk the few blocks to the Manic Pixie Dream House (ugh) to see if someone was around to share a cup of hot chocolate and listen to her complain.

(Chauv was rarely in when she called by, to the point that Viola didn't even bother to go to the upper floor any more, though there was usually a book or a t-shirt to steal from Sage, to make the trip worthwhile.)

Still, she had a point to make: Hebe was never there.

"I know," said Hebe with an awkward laugh. "You know how it is. Real life. Not Real real, just… ordinary job stuff. It's hard to keep up with everyone. We're never in the same place at the same time."

"You should come to their stupid game nights," Viola said, eyeing a pair of particularly soft cushions the same shade as Medusa's glaze. "That's what they're for. Since when does Dec supply homeware shops?"

"That's how I found this place," said Hebe. "Or, how it found me, I suppose. Aurora loves Dec's work, she leased some of his statues for window displays, and…" she shrugged and smiled, more awkward than this conversation really deserved. Viola wondered why. "Here I am."

"Are you and Dec fucking?" Viola asked before thinking about it.

Hebe blushed hard, and looked quietly horrified. Then she lifted her chin. "That's not really any of your business."

"Fair point," says Viola. *So, no, then. Or maybe, not yet.*

"It's complicated."

"Not especially." Viola shook her head. "I'm not going to turn you to stone."

That, at least, made Hebe laugh. "I'd forgotten you're nice sometimes."

"Maybe because you see an angry gorgon version of me at work every day." Viola rolled her eyes. "You should go to their stupid game night," she said again. "They miss you."

Hebe bit her lip. "You're right. I didn't mean to stay away so long. I just wanted a bit of space to figure myself out without all the noise."

"Believe me," said Viola. "I get it. Look how far I went."

"OMG," said Hebe, and there she was, that same little nerd with the big eyes who seduced Ferd with her weird down-to-earth normality. "I can't believe I didn't ask you about Paris! How was it?"

"It was *everything*," said Viola. And, perhaps because she

knew Hebe wasn't spending much time around the rest of the group these days, she found herself confessing the thing she hasn't said to any of them. Not yet. "I can't wait to go back. For good, maybe."

———

SEPTEMBER

- Thesis.
- Rinse.
- Repeat.

———

"Elvish," Viola said, not quite believing it. "*Elvish*?"

Professor M leaned back in her chair, regarding Viola with her steady green-eyed gaze. "I think you'll find that a great deal of scholarship on Prometheus and the origins of magic was published in the 1970s in a variety of obscure Elvish journals that you do not appear to have referred to in your footnotes."

"Those papers have never been translated," said Viola. "And they're fifty years old..." Also, she had thought she had gotten away with not having to learn bloody Elvish.

"Nevertheless. A doctoral thesis is expected to demonstrate a wide reading across the entire chosen subject." Professor Medeous tapped the desk with a single burgundy fingernail. "You don't want your examiners to be asking themselves the question, 'Does she even know about the Elvish papers?' do you?"

Viola closed her eyes for just a moment and imagined the entire university bursting into flames: orange and purple and all shades of scorched earth.

"Elvish," she said in a voice that was remarkably steady

given the circumstances. "All right, then. I guess I'd better learn Elvish."

———

OCTOBER

The hex wig is a bit much, but Viola couldn't resist it when she saw it in the window of the costume shop. The snakes come 'alive' and wriggle around hissing when you say the keyword *fierce* out loud.

It's stupid, but she's been looking forward to this all week. She's been moving from library to library, grinding through the latest wave of corrections. She's so tired, she never wants to look at another book again.

Why did she think there was a future for her in academia?

So yeah, she's been hanging out all week to show off her stupid snake wig at game night.

Medusa was supposed to be a one-shot villain, but Viola's first appearance last month worked well with the storyline. Mei added more backstory and character connections for the next session. Viola has a suspicion that the plan is to 'redeem' Medusa and have her eventually join the main party as a regular player character.

She's going to have to say no. (She doesn't want to say no.) She honestly can't commit to coming every week. And after December, well… everything's going to be different.

———

"AND, BACK BY POPULAR ACCLAIM, MEDUSA, THE SNAKE-HEADED GORGON!"

"Omg."

"Vi."

"Vale."

"That is amazing."

It's embarrassing how much she needed this. It's not embarrassing at all how fabulous she looks in a wig of live snakes. She's gonna murder them all.

So fun.

———

"We're not children, Mei!"

"And yet the lockbox for your phones was necessary. Fifteen minute break *only*, people, we have a ravine to burn down."

Sage and Viola reach for their phones at the same time — she sees immediately she has three missed calls from France, visible on her screen. Their eyes meet briefly, and she makes a run for it.

"Just getting some air, I'll be back!"

"You'd better be!" Mei yells after her.

———

So here she is, sitting in the little backyard, still wearing her Medusa wig, frantically trying to connect a call to The Academie des Sorcières. Finally she reaches Emil at the desk — why are they even working on what must be Saturday morning for them — and gets put through to Professeur Poitiers.

The conversation is brief, but informative, and it's only after she has disconnected that Viola feels Sage nearby, his magic sparking against her own. Fire and fire.

"You don't have to eavesdrop," she calls out. "You can just ask."

"I didn't hear what you were saying," he grumbles, but comes to sit next to her, passing her a can of Beltaine. She got addicted to this stuff in France. Unlike lemon croissants and all the best cheeses, you can buy it here.

"You can ask," she says again, more gently.

Sage shrugs. "Not much to ask. It's obvious they'd want you

back. Belladonna U is too small for you, Viola Vale. The world is your shark chum."

"It feels weird to be thinking about job offers when I'm not done yet," she says, testing out the idea aloud.

"Like you're not gonna do brilliantly. Come on."

"It still feels... too soon."

"Never too soon to think about your career."

She eyes him suspiciously; there's something about his tone. "How's Honours going, Sage? There was a bidding war for you, wasn't there? I hope Dem Thaum Phen is working out."

He gives her a savage, biting smile. "Bit late to change my mind, isn't it?"

Viola keeps pressing; she's not sure why, as he clearly isn't comfortable talking about it. But who else is he going to talk to about this? She's the only one of all of them who has kept going this far into academia. "Are you going to continue on? Get your doctorate?"

"Not at this university." This time it sounds more like a snarl.

Viola blinks, surprised. "Sage."

"Forget it."

"What's going on?"

"You don't have time for this shit, it's fine."

"It's not fine." A cold feeling spreads over her. "Is this something to do with — you know. New Year's?" She'd left the country to get away from the stares and the looks. She was reasonably cushioned in her own department, because Professor M never had time for all the Basilisk Board politicking, and she was such an institution in the Department of the Real, she got away with it. Viola's own father and Jules' mother and grandfather weren't exactly the cuddliest of allies, but they turned against the Chauvelins the second it was revealed that their actions risked their own heirs.

No one has even mentioned the Chauvelin scandal to Viola, since she returned from France. She knows there have to be members of the Board who are angry at how the Chauvelins were brought down, but she's been protected from any petty acts of bureaucratic vengeance.

If she'd given any thought to how the arrest of the Chauvelins might affect Sage, she might have assumed he was in a similar position. But that was her forgetting her privilege again, wasn't it? Sage didn't have the same support system Viola did.

The snobby Department of Demonstrative Thaumaturgical Phenomena had been willing to overlook Sage's 'colourful background' and lack of Basilisk breeding because he was brilliant. But was it enough to protect him?

(Surely Jules would have told her, if Sage was having trouble at uni. But she hasn't seen Jules in ages. Chauv. She has to talk to Chauv. If only they could have had this conversation in two months time, when she had time to follow up properly.)

"How's Professor Fordyce as a supervisor?" she tries.

Sage stands up, holding out a hand to pull her to her feet. "They got rid of him," he says calmly. "No loss. Don't worry, Vale. I won't go down so easily." He drops a kiss on the top of her head. "Seriously. Put it out of your head. You have a thesis to finish."

"So do you," she says pointedly. An Honours thesis is a fraction of a doctorate, but it's not *nothing*.

Sage shrugs. "The world's bigger than Belladonna U. Isn't it?"

———

NOVEMBER

- Footnotes.
- Semi-colons.
- Headers and footers.
- Do I need to completely re-write chapter three?
- Thesis meetings.
- More fucking footnotes.

Don't read the job offers

- Calls from Paris.

Don't think about Paris.

- Worry about Sage

you don't have time to think about Sage

- Messages to Ferdinand Chauvelin that he ignores: all of them.

————

DECEMBER

"Viola...."

"Vale Vale Vale."

"Viooooooolllllla."

"Maybe she can't hear us."

"Oh, she can hear us."

(Sound of a window flying up)

"You. Arseholes."

"She heard us!"

"It is the night before my thesis is due. The night before. I have six hours to check every fucking comma. What on earth do you two clowns want that is so important?"

"We want you to come out and play."

"Nightshade, you knob. That's not gonna convince her."

"No, you're drunk."

"I am shutting this window."

"Wait. Vale. Viola. This is important. So important."

"Chauv, you've barely spoken a word to me all year. Jules

has ghosted me for months. What exactly can be so important that you need my attention now, right now, on the most important night of my career?"

"We have to save Belladonna U."

"And Sage."

"I think possibly we have to save Belladonna U *from Sage*."

(Long pause)

"Hold my broom for me. I'm coming out the window."

CHAPTER FIVE
THE YEAR OF JUNIPER

JANUARY

FROM THE DIARY OF MISS JUNIPER CRESSWELL,
RECENTLY GRADUATED WITCH

My mother has never looked so frail. Clover Cresswell's
naturally green hair is washed out; her cheeks are hollow. She
can barely raise her voice above a whisper, even to complain
about how sore her throat is, how tired she is.

"I think she was cursed," says Carmen, home for a summer
visit but due back to her job at the Floating Orchestra any day
now. "The new neighbours are hags, and she's always picking
fights with them."

"She wasn't cursed," says our father for the fortieth time,
irritated at being pulled away from whatever enchanted concerto
he is composing in the attic. "She over-stretched herself working
on her last album. I told her she was pouring too much personal
energy into the bass line."

"Cursed," mouths Calypso, the youngest, already packed for
her own trip to Melbourne, ready to start at Belladonna U.

(Semester doesn't start for another seven weeks but no one suggests she might stick around to take care of their mother…)

This is what I returned to. This is where I am now.

I realised how this would go as soon as I walked into the family home and saw my mother wanly laid out on the couch, sucking on barley sugars.

(I was only supposed to stay here for a week.)

(I promised myself no longer than a week.)

Foolishly, I returned to the Cresswell family home without an escape plan; I graduated last month and have not yet secured a job as an excuse to stay in Melbourne, far from the spooky sandstone house in small town Tasmania where my family has spent the last six generations making music, magic, and each other miserable.

"That's settled, then," says my father, as if there was an actual discussion. "Juniper will stay and look after you."

He kisses his wife absently on the top of her head and wanders away, humming to himself.

Just like that, I'm stuck. I'm the frog in the cauldron. It's boiling and boiling, but I don't hop out, not because I'm too stupid to know when a cauldron will scald me to death, but because someone's nailed my flipper to the base of the cauldron.

No, I don't think I am being over-dramatic. And even if I was, that's what a diary is *for*!

FEBRUARY

"OMG are you Juniper Cresswell?"

Juniper froze. Nothing to see here. Just picking lettuce from the garden. Her mother, still recuperating from her (probably-not-a-curse) creative exhaustion, was determined to eat nothing but salads during the day.

"Yes?" Juniper ventured.

A head stuck up from over the top of a passionfruit trellis, showing a shock of blue hair and a very enthusiastic face. "You're the cellist from Fake Geek Girl!"

"Um, yes." She had never been randomly recognised in public before, not unless you counted music festival stalkers who tried to steal her body.

"I LOVE YOU!" The face bounced again, then steadied against the fence. She was somewhere between 12 and 15 years old, and very high pitched. "I picked the cello at school because of you. Are the rest of Fake Geek Girl here? Why are you in Tasmania?"

Juniper blinked a lot, then smiled and started answering questions. As they chatted, she picked her lettuce leaves so she could make a quick retreat if she needed to.

(There would be no hugging. She had learned her lesson about drawing physical boundaries with people who loved the band.)

But it was nice to see a friendly face.

Also to be reminded that, actually, she was in a band.

———

MARCH

"I don't know why you're being so difficult," sighed her mother.

Juniper handed over the third cup of tea she had made that morning. "I'm not being difficult," she said calmly. "I don't want the audition."

"Do you know how rarely a cello position opens up?"

Juniper stared at her feet, then caught herself. No. She wouldn't do this. "I don't want to play the cello in an orchestra. I'm honestly not good enough to play at that level, with all that pressure. I would be miserable."

If she had learned anything from her years at Belladonna U, her years in Fake Geek Girl, her years around Holly, the most

shameless person she had ever met… it was that she was
allowed to choose things that made her happy.

"You don't know what you want," her mother said
dismissively.

Juniper smiled. "I like music," she said. "But I don't want to
make it my job."

She'd known what she wanted for a long time. It was saying
those things out loud that took all the effort.

———

APRIL

> JUNIPER: Is Holly OK?

> HEBE: ??

> JUNIPER: I've been getting some odd texts
> from her, and she just called and sounded sort
> of… never mind. It's probably nothing.

> HEBE: I haven't seen her for ages. I should call.

> JUNIPER: are you not… one room away
> from her?

> HEBE: funny story

———

> MISSJUNIPERCRESS HAS OPENED THIS
> MIRRORCHAT

> MISSJUNIPERCRESS: I booked a flight back in
> 2 weeks, have you rented out Hebe's room yet?
> Can I stay with you until I find a place?

> MEICAKES: finding a new roommate I don't know fills me with horror and dread. Want to like, come stay forever?

> MISSJUNIPERCRESS: um, yes please

———

MAY

FROM THE PERSONAL, HAND-WRITTEN DIARY OF MISS JUNIPER CRESSWELL: SLIGHTLY CONFUSED WITCH

Things have shifted with Holly.

First there were all those odd texts last month about cryptids and song lyrics, while Holly put herself back together after being temporarily distracted by the wrong job and the wrong boyfriend.

Then I came home and we moved in together.

I mean, I moved in with Mei and Holly, into Hebe's old room, but... we were living together.

And texting all the time.

And I started to think...

Here's the thing. I am not the one with massive self-confidence. I'm not going to assume someone likes me just because there are moments, and smiles, and because she seems embarrassed around me sometimes, which suggests the universe is actually upside down and inside out.

But.

I think maybe Holly likes me.

And I actually don't know what to do about it.

———

JUNE

FROM THE PERSONAL, HAND-WRITTEN DIARY OF MISS
JUNIPER CRESSWELL: RECENTLY EMPLOYED WITCH

When in doubt, admin.

My mother always said I'd do rather well in admin. I think
she meant it to be insulting — *not that there's anything wrong
with box office, darling, if you can't make it to the orchestra —*
but she wasn't wrong. I'm calm and well-organised and I don't
hate making phone calls.

I studied Unreal Arts, and devoted all my spare time to
music while being determined not to have a career in music.
Admin was always my destiny. I didn't major in political science
for nothing, though — I was hoping for something in government. I saw myself as the assistant to some glamorous, high-
achieving female politician, making life easier for her while she
changed the world.

Unfortunately, I didn't get interviews for those jobs. The job
interview I got was for the third office assistant to an MP who,
I'm pretty sure, would vote for a baby-eating bill if he thought it
might make him look sufficiently manly in public.

It occurs to me that I should probably not be writing this
down. I wouldn't want my diary to become Exhibit A when my
boss becomes inevitably involved in some kind of horrifying
scandal.

[*Several discreet magical coding spells later*]

Yes, my new boss. Hecate help me, I took the job.

It's possible I should just… stop keeping a diary for a while.

Or only write about personal things.

Like how Holly has ended sleeping over in my bed three
times this month after long late-night chats.

I hope…

I think…

No, I'm not writing that down.

———

JULY

Juniper hated being alone in the office. At least when Mariel and Tim were there, Ogden Locksley MP would shout his commands at them, and ignore her, unless coffee was required.

When she was alone he would stare at her as if he had forgotten she existed, call her by the wrong name, and expect her to know absolutely every file or paper that had passed through Mariel or Tim's hands in the last twelve months.

It was terrifying. But only one of them had to be here on Saturdays when His Nibs insisted on coming in, and it was her turn.

At least today Locksley was holed up in his office, shouting into phones and mirrors simultaneously, and had not so far noticed her horrible mistake.

"Your delivery, madame?"

Jules Nightshade lounged in the doorway, holding a large manila envelope.

"You angel!" said Juniper, relief flooding her. She ran forward, snatched it from him, checked the contents, and then hugged him. "You saved my bacon."

She still couldn't believe she had accidentally taken those papers home, let alone leaving them on her bedside table when she left for work today. She could get into so much trouble, taking anything out of the office.

(Almost like she had other things on her mind)

(Almost like she had woken up with Holly's hair in her mouth, again, after yet another friendly but not quite romantic sleepover together.)

"Hang on," said Juniper. "I asked Mei to bring these."

"Mei is Broomdashing, Sage and Holly are in the middle of some kind of project, and I haven't seen hide nor hair of Dec or Chauv. It's only me, I'm afraid, darling. Coming to the rescue."

"I appreciate it," she said fervently. And then, because she rather liked that she and Jules were at this level of friendship now: "Things going well with Sage, then?"

"Shut up shut up," he said, smiling brightly. "I hope they let you off early enough for Cake Wizards tonight."

"Me too. I think maybe we'll get to meet the Sorbet Queen this week."

The door slammed open behind them, and to Juniper's horror, Ogden Gulliver MP strolled out of his office. "January, do you have those Fisher numbers?"

"I do," she said, discreetly sliding them out of the envelope and handing them to him.

Ogden stopped, staring at Jules. "Young Nightshade. Not your neck of the woods, is it? How's your Dad?"

"I imagine you've seen him more recently than me," said Jules, oozing Basilisk charm.

"Ha, yes! Probably. Tell West I owe him a game of troll snooker." Ogden frowned slightly. "Are you wanting to bend my ear? Really should make an appointment. Jacaranda, can we get Mr Nightshade into the appointment book for next week?"

"No need," said Jules smoothly. "I was just about to take Juniper here out to lunch."

Ogden blinked and looked at Juniper like it had just occurred to him she might be a person. "It's three in the afternoon."

"Shamefully late to be taking her break, but she's such a hard worker," said Jules.

"Uh, yes. Might as well head off for the day, Juniper. I'm going home myself in a minute."

"Excellent," said Jules, smiling with all of his teeth. "Enjoy the rest of the weekend. Locksley."

"You too, Nightshade."

———

"What was that?" Juniper said as they left the office a few minutes later, hand in hand.

"He's friends with my dad," said Jules, gritting his teeth.

"Whole family is. Horrible toads, the lot of them. Want a lift back to the house?"

"Oh no," said Juniper, squeezing his hand. "I am totally buying you lunch."

AUGUST

Holly had been talking about the new song, and Sage's plans for the band, for the last thirty minutes without stopping.

Juniper found it soothing, how little she was expected to contribute. There wasn't even space to make 'ooh' and 'ah' noises, or to nod in a supportive manner.

She might close her eyes and take a nap, except that Holly was electric like this, all spark and snap and pretty eyes.

Juniper listened for as long as she could, until Holly finally, finally, wound to a close.

"So what do you think?" asked Holly, breathless.

Juniper kissed her.

SEPTEMBER

"You look exhausted," Juniper said to Jules.

"Thank you, darling," he replied. "Nice to know my eye-cream is failing to perform miracles."

Meeting up for lunch every few weeks was a thing that they did now. She wasn't sure exactly where he worked, but it seemed to be near enough to her office to make things convenient.

Jules had missed the last Cake Wizards session, and looked miserable when Juniper asked about it...

"Should I be worried?" she asked.

He stabbed a fork into his panini, which was entirely the wrong way to eat paninis. "Don't worry about me, darling. I'm bulletproof. Tell me about your job."

"I work for an MP, Jules. Actual daily details are all top secret."

An odd look crossed his face. "I know *that*. Is your boss still a colossal dickhead?"

"Obviously." And she told him a story about Ogden's terrible behaviour in the office staff tea room.

By the end of it, she had coaxed two smiles out of him.

———

OCTOBER

"I've never been to an orchestra before," said Holly, whose hair was bright pink for the occasion. It looked dramatic over a tuxedo jacket and tiny white dress.

Calypso Cresswell, settling into her seat on the other side of Juniper, looked startled. "Are you not a musical person, then?" she asked, in a sharp voice that made her sound exactly like Carmen.

Holly blinked. "I'm in a band," she said.

"Oh." Juniper's little sister rolled her eyes, as only a first year uni student could; totally dismissive.

"Your *sister's* band," Holly followed up.

"Are you still doing that, Juniper?" Calypso ran her eye over the programme. "Oh, look, Carmen has three solos!"

"We have a show coming up on New Year's Eve," Holly added, sounding cranky now. "New venue. You should come." Her tone now said: *I dare you to say yes*.

"I'll probably have other invitations," shrugged Calypso. "I did go out to see a band the other week, actually."

Juniper was surprised at that. "Really?" It was rare for

anyone in her family to listen to anything that wasn't played by people in suits.

"On Friday night, at Medea's Cauldron. They're called Null."

"Oh," said Holly, who had taken the loss of the regular gig at Medea's Cauldron quite hard. "Them."

"Shh," said Calypso. "It's starting!"

———

NOVEMBER

Juniper slipped silently out of Holly's bed in her long vintage nightgown. She would get dressed in her own room. There was no reason to wake up her girlfriend (girlfriend!) just because she had to be at work stupidly early.

A dark shape on the couch stirred, and Juniper pushed down a scream. "Jules?"

"Shhh."

He sat up suddenly. His magic was a muffled presence wrapped in stale coffee. His hair was wild; his eyes worse. "Juniper."

"What is going on?" she hissed.

"Um. I can't tell you."

Juniper let out a small growl. She was rather proud of it.

"Sorry. Sorry. It's just — literal national secrets. I shouldn't tell you anything. But I didn't want you to go in blind."

"In blind where?"

He looked like such a wreck. She wanted to put a blanket over him.

"Juniper," Jules said seriously. "If I tell you something, can you pretend you don't know?"

"Have you met me? I've been secretive and repressed my whole life. No one ever knows what's going on inside my head."

He blinked, listing slightly to one side. "I just assume you're constantly narrating your own life as if you're in a Jane Austen novel."

Juniper frowned at him. "That's quite a lucky guess, for a gentleman clearly lacking in sleep."

Jules sighed, rubbing gunk from his eyes. "Okay. Here we go. Your boss was arrested last night."

Juniper wished she could even pretend to be surprised. "That must have been quite the sex scandal, if he couldn't successfully buy off the police."

"Actually nothing to do with his creepy sex life, about which the least said the better. He's, uh. There's this whole international warlock consortium of evil, and…" Jules broke off, looking helpless. "I shouldn't say more than that. The more you know, the more complicit you might look."

"Then why are you here?"

"Because… you're about to have a really bad day in the office. People from *my* office are going to ask you a lot of questions." He trailed off, sounding helpless. "It made more sense in my head."

Juniper leaned in and gave him the world's biggest hug. "You're such an idiot. Won't you be in trouble at work for sneaking off to spill national secrets to me?"

He had never told her what he did for a living, but she had some idea. She was one of life's observers, after all.

"Sage is on official record as my boyfriend," he muttered into her flannel-clad shoulder. "Won't look weird, me coming to the house. But they already know I know Ogden. And you. Had to mention you when I disclosed he's a friend of my dad's."

"For the record, when did you last see said boyfriend? Follow up question, when did you last get a full night's sleep?"

"S'been a while." He sounded half unconscious already.

"Right. Well, if they ask either of us tomorrow where you spent the night, it would be better if we didn't have to lie about it."

Juniper stood up, hauling Jules to his feet. He followed her obediently, out of the flat, up the internal staircase, and directly into the kitchen of the upper floor of the Manic Pixie Dream House, because the boys were lazy about security.

She walked Jules all the way to Sage's bedroom, and knocked on the door.

"Urgh," she heard from inside, which was enough to have her opening the door, and pushing Jules inside.

"Please look after this Jules," Juniper said sweetly. "I have a busy day ahead of me, and I need to know he's in good hands."

Sage, mussed and half asleep, stuck his head up off the pillow. When he saw Jules lurching in his general direction, he gave a slow, sleepy smile and pushed the doona back in a vaguely welcoming manner.

"About fucken time," he grunted. "Where have you been?"

———

So, Juniper's terrible boss was running a sideline in sharing national secrets with an international warlock consortium of evil. More importantly, if he had been arrested, that meant he might not be in the office for the foreseeable future.

Juniper would answer all the questions the government liked, if there was half a chance of trading in her boss for a competent replacement.

Today might be the day to see if she could pull off a power suit.

———

DECEMBER

Dear Diary,

I can write in you again because my new job is at a dental magician's office and nothing is likely to happen to require you to become an exhibit in a court case.

I haven't performed in public in more than a year.

We've been practicing, of course, and we recorded a few vids. We're completely ready for this next stage of Fake Geek Girl. Sage is so invested in this New Year's performance.

The plan makes sense. Big comeback show, then we finalise the new album, crowdfund it, start our adult musical careers. There are spreadsheets. Timelines. Amazingly, Holly has done most of the paperwork.

But it's been a long year, and I forgot how hard stagefright hits me.

Things have been amazing lately with me and Holly, our relationship. I'm happy. But am I filling a void for her? Am I just a placeholder while she figures out her music career, her relationship with her sister, her friends?

Wait one moment, she's trying to get my attention.

————

"Hey Junie."

"Hi."

"How do I look? You look amazing."

"Thank you. I love your hair like that, very punk."

"This is going to be good, right? It's not a colossal embarrassing mistake."

"If it is, then it's a colossal, embarrassing mistake we're making together."

(Kissing sound)

"Can we talk, Junie, after the show?"

"Uh, no!"

"What?"

"Holly, you're the one who keeps telling me to stand up for myself. If you really mean that, you can't *do* things like saying you need to talk right before the most important performance of our career. If you want to break up with me…"

"No! Of course not."

"Well, good."

"The opposite of that. Really."

"Oh. That's nice. The opposite of a breakup. That's not going to… Sorry, I need more of a definition of what exactly you mean by that."

"Juniper, I am totally ready to do that. I am prepared. But there's a whole speech and a song, and we literally do not have time right now."

"There's a song?"

"It's unrehearsed."

"It sounds like we should… talk, after the show."

"That's what I said in the first place!"

"Right. Good."

(*Kissing sound*)

"WILL YOU TWO GET ON STAGE?"

CHAPTER SIX
THE YEAR OF HOLLY

JANUARY

Lyrics notebook: empty pages

———

FEBRUARY

Lyrics notebook: empty pages

———

MARCH

Lyrics notebook: empty pages

———

APRIL

I forgot how to be a freaking unicorn
Show me how
I know you remember
Show me now

———

MAY

Her hair is like
Cello music

———

JUNE

Late night
Talking
Can't stop
Writing songs about
That girl in my band
This is getting
Self-referential
Make it stop
(Don't stop)

———

JULY

SAGEPLAYSTHEDRUMS HAS OPENED THIS
MIRRORCHAT

SagePlaysTheDrums: Hol, typing the words 'her hair smells nice' ten times into a Word Document is not a love song. It's not even a song.

SagePlaysTheDrums: ask her out already this is getting old

———

AUGUST

> *How did you get so brave*
> *I'm still writing a song*
> *About how to kiss you*
> *How did you get there first?*

———

> *I'm pretty sure*
> *You're some kind of superhero*

———

You're so brave
[You probably think this song is about you] lyric
redacted

———

SEPTEMBER

"Holly…"

"No. I draw the line at games with dice, Junie."

"Want to see a drawing of me as my character?"

"I saw that drawing already, it's cute but it's mostly cats."

"War felines. I call them the Creme Pat Cats. My character conjures them from a magical sword."

"Too much cat, not enough Juniper."

———

OCTOBER

HOLLYRULESTHE WORLD HAS OPENED THIS MIRRORCHAT

HollyRulesThe World: where are u

HollyRulesThe World: also I kind of hate you today

HollyRulesThe World: hebebebebebebebe

> HebeIsSoBoring: I wrote a song

HollyRulesThe World: WHAT TELL ME EVERYTHING CAN I HEART IT

HollyRulesThe World: I MEAN HEAR IT BUT ALSO HEART IT PROBABLY

HollyRulesThe World: ps I haz a super hot girlfriend

> HebeIsSoBoring: WHAT TELL ME EVERYTHING

———

NOVEMBER

HOLLYRULESTHE WORLD HAS OPENED THIS MIRRORCHAT

HollyRulesThe World: we have enough songs for this New Year's concert, right? We can pull something amazing together. It has to be amazing, we can't just turn up and be exactly the same

SagePlaysTheDrums: got any new material?

SagePlaysTheDrums: I mean, obviously we can do it

SagePlaysTheDrums: but also, write a fucking song that's not about your perfect relationship, Holly

HollyRulesThe World: I'm not writing a song about your Cake Wizards game

SagePlaysTheDrums: Juniper would make out with you so hard if you did

HollyRulesThe World: HA joke's on you, she does that anyway

———

DECEMBER

HOLLYRULESTHE WORLD HAS OPENED THIS MIRRORCHAT

HollyRulesThe World: I told Juniper the thing

HebeIsSoBoring: did she like your song?

HollyRulesThe World: she said it back even before I got to the song

HebeIsSoBoring: high pitched squee

HollyRulesThe World: !!!

HebeIsSoBoring: !!!! Btw your show was amazing tonight

HollyRulesThe World: you came?

HebeIsSoBoring: duh

HollyRulesThe World: are you still here?

HebeIsSoBoring: I haven't got to congratulate my awesome sister yet, so yes I'm here, obviously

HebeIsSoBoring: over at the bar, you can't miss me, I'm with Sage

HebeIsSoBoring: though fans keep coming over to ask him to sign body parts & Jules is about ready to caveman him out of here

HebeIsSoBoring: it's OK I can see you tomorrow, you'll be busy with Juniper

HollyRulesThe World: shut up, wait right there, we're coming to find you

CHAPTER SEVEN
THE YEAR OF SAGE

JANUARY

Medea's Cauldron is hopping for a Friday night and for once, I'm not on stage, or taking a break, or worrying about my bloody drum kit.

I'm at an overcrowded table near the bar, nursing a beer and feeling like shit.

"Hey," says Hebe, leaning into me so she can be heard over the sound of Null, the new The Band that's taken over our old Friday night slot. (Not sure what's going on there: it's a bit punk, a bit industrial, lots of deep breathing from the lead singer, not enough lyrics.) "At least you'll have more time for Honours. I'm sure it's going to be a lot of work."

"For you too," I say back, because I'm an arsehole. I'm like, 95% sure Hebe has quit uni and isn't telling us yet.

She gives me an awkward smile which makes me feel like, ten times more shit than before. "A lot's going to change this year."

"Nah," I say, and drop my arm around her shoulders. "More of the same."

———

FEBRUARY

"Mei, I don't have time to fall in love with another freaking anime series."

Classic last words.

———

MARCH

Professor Fordyce, with his leather jackets and rolled-up sleeves, is just as distractingly hot as ever.

No, shut up, that's not why I picked him as an Honours supervisor.

There are three of us under him in Dem Thaum Phen this year, a big-eyed girl in glasses who just transferred from Nimue University in the UK, and Dinesh — who's been in half my classes since I first started at Belladonna U. (I don't think we've ever talked to each other — this year we've upgraded to manly nods.)

So three of us, sprawled out in a seminar room designed for 30. That leaves plenty of space for Fordyce to stride around, making one of his speeches.

Bloke stepped up for us at New Year's. I've gotta lotta time for him. But man, he likes his speeches.

"Magic is supposed to be dangerous," he says now, prowling around in front of us, like he's trying to catch the attention of a lecture hall full of bored first years. "I'm sure you're already thinking about your topics for the thesis that will form a third of this year's final grade…"

Nope. Inspiration has not yet hit. It's the first day, mate, settle down.

"…and I'm sure other professors would caution you to

choose wisely. Consider areas of study with substantial grant support. Collaborate. Add something to a currently-popular theory so as to prepare yourself for a well-funded Masters or Doctorate next year. A safe career move."

Next year. It's barely even this year. I discreetly cast an eyeball in the direction of each of my fellow Hons students. Ms Big Eyes is scribbling notes. Dinesh looks wary. Or hungry. I've never been able to read him.

"However!" Fordyce roars, building up to something. "This is Demonstrative Thaumaturgical Phenomena. There's no such thing as a safe field of study. We take risks. We experiment. We ask the questions of magic that no one else asks, and then we make it bend to our will."

So, Professor Fordyce is having a nervous breakdown. Possibly, the authorities should be called. But I've never been one for authorities. Plus, the crazy eyes look kinda suits him.

"Ask yourself!" he continues. "How can I change the field of magic forever?"

Almost immediately he turns around, writing names on the blackboard of paradigm-smashing witches and warlocks of history. To inspire us, I guess.

I ease my phone out of my pocket, and chuck a text to Mei:

> SAGE: when's the first session? I feel the need for some Cake Wizards tomfoolery

> MEI: this Sat. U better be there! Planned your character yet?

> SAGE: thinking pirate captain

> MEI: this is 100% a land campaign

> SAGE: yes AND

> MEI: we'll make it work.

APRIL

"So this is a thing now," I say, as Jules follows me upstairs after our latest Cake Wizards session, and kisses me against the door-frame of the kitchen.

"Do you want it to be?" asks Jules, all lazy drawl and limbs.

"We used to fight more before we got to the good part."

We used to put up resistance.

Somewhere along the way, this month, we got comfortable with each other instead.

(*You'd make a good boyfriend if you just let yourself,* I hear Hebe telling me.)

"Shut up and come to bed," says Jules, already on his way to my room.

And, yeah. Why the fuck not?

———

MAY

"You didn't have to come," says Ferd, looking sick as a dog.

"You know me, any excuse to wear a suit." I'm not wearing a suit. I'm wearing my favourite Kraken t-shirt, the one I stole back from Vale before she left the country. It's deeply inappropriate for court, but I'm not the one who has to go on the witness stand.

I *am* a witness. We were all witnesses to the fuckery that went down on New Year's Day. But Nightshade's mother has the world's sharkiest lawyer, he's basically made of gold-plated pin stripes. Blood diamonds running in his veins. You get the idea. He's expensive.

The caviar lawyer didn't want any of us ratbag students harshing his vibe, so our testimony was pre-recorded, mounted on enchanted mirrors, and cross-charmed for verity.

The only witnesses to take the stand are the defendants themselves, Ferd's parents. It's the first time he's seen them since it all went down.

Ferd doesn't need to be here. Jules sure as hell didn't turn up, and Vale is conveniently still far away in the land of chocolate croissants and hot Frenchmen.

For some reason, Ferd wants to be here to witness the final scene of this colossal shitshow and I'd be ten kinds of arsehole to let him come alone.

The final speeches — shark lawyer against shark lawyer — are works of art.

When the settlement amount is announced, I can't take my eyes off Irene Nightshade. She's perfectly still, perfectly poised, and I can feel the icy chill of her magic from all the way back here in the cheap seats.

She smiles very briefly — the tiniest tweak of her lipstick — like a satisfied vampire that just finished eating the prettiest people in the room.

She's terrifying in victory.

It's like a little glimpse of the future of what Jules might be like in 25 years time.

So that's something to look forward to.

JUNE

"I need a job," Holly announces, throwing herself on my bed so that it bounces several times.

Jules groans and puts a pillow over his head. Somehow it works — he's fast asleep again before the bed even settles from Holly's extra weight.

I blink at the too-much-light that Holly brought with her. She hasn't even opened the curtains. She's sort of glowing.

(She's been doing that a lot lately, since Juniper moved in downstairs)

"What the fuck, Hol," I groan. "Knock first. We could have been having sex."

"If you were, it wasn't with Jules, he's clearly asleep." So much perkiness in one body. How can she sleep at night? Oh, wait. It's 11:30pm and she's not asleep.

Clearly I'm not getting to sleep either until I unpack whatever it is she's vibrating about.

"Spill," I mutter.

"I need a job, I told you. I chucked in my soul destroying job to write this album and it's good, it's going well, I think, but I'm running out of ramen and Juniper will never fall in love with me if I don't cover my part of the rent every month, so..."

"So what, you want suggestions?"

"Yes! Jobs I can get that won't suck up all of my album writing time."

"Couldn't you Broomdash like Mei?" Too late, I forget who I'm talking to. Holly needs to be kept away from broomsticks for the sake of the country.

"Broomsticks are for losers," she says airily. "Next."

"Um. Admin? Retail?"

"Juniper has one of those admin jobs and it takes her WHOLE DAY. Customer service jobs are so hard on the feet, plus I always get fired from them after like, three weeks. There's so much paperwork. I tried asking around a bunch of the local places anyway, but this is a university district, so all the stupid students have sucked up all the shifts. Can't you just get me a job wherever you work?"

I wait a beat. "Hol. Where do you think I work?"

She waits too, crumpling her nose. "Huh. Wait. No. What? Isn't it like... a cool giant record store that sells vintage vinyl?"

"No, that's a movie you're thinking of. From the 90s. Before you were born."

"Bartender? Barista. High Court Judge? Gym instructor. Underwear model?"

"Remember how I sold a song to Kraken last year? And it did really well?"

Holly's mouth falls open. She's like a cartoon dancemoji indicating awe and shock. "You're still living off that?"

"It was a good song. There's money in music sometimes."

"What the fuck, Sage. How did I not know this? Shouldn't you be saving it for your old age?"

I shrug. "Thought it was worth doing the full time student thing this year. Honours and all. Plus I thought I'd need time for Fake Geek Girl. If we ever get back to regular band practice, you'll be glad I'm not spending 40 hours a week on a construction site."

Holly considers this. "Could I work construction?"

"Not safely. You're a flailer."

"Are you writing more songs for Kraken?"

"I've got like three in the pipeline. It'll probably never happen again."

Holly looks outraged. "They can't have those songs, Sage. We have an album to put together. Those could be *our* zillions!"

"Will my songs even fit on your new album? They're not about cryptids or pretty girls who play cellos…"

"I'm going job hunting now," she says sulkily, flouncing off the bed.

"Good. Bye!"

"Or maybe I'll just sell a kickass song to a band with a higher profile than ours!"

"We haven't updated our Youtube page in months, Hol. Every band has a higher profile than ours."

JULY

Holly is fire.

My magic fills her shape, burning for an infinite moment.

There's a buzzing sound, and the flame falters, dies out.

We're both standing ankle-deep in the ornamental lake on the Belladonna U campus, back to reality.

Holly slides her hand-mirror out of a pocket. "It's Juniper. She left some work shit at home, it's urgent, and Mei is out Broomdashing. Can we come back to this later?"

I can feel it, the shape of the spell, burning under my finger-nails. I so almost have it right. This is the spell I need to complete my thesis. To finally prove... "Jules is at home, hang on."

I call him quickly, pass on Juniper's urgent request. "One more time?"

"Well, fine," Holly sighs. "But at least take a pic. Me on fire would look amazing on our next album cover."

———

AUGUST

"Vale."

"Sage."

A rare sighting of Viola Vale, postgrad student, a few months from thesis submission. Where else? The library.

She looks busy and frazzled, and she's about to pass by...

"Wait. Please. For a minute?" I sound whiny as hell.

She rolls her eyes. "Sage, I don't have time to talk about Jules, or Chauv, or whatever's going on at that chaos house of yours."

"I need to talk about Pandora."

That makes her pause. Vale's been working on her own thesis about the mythical origins of magic for as long as I've known her.

"Buy me a hot chocolate and I'll give you fifteen minutes," she says, and then disappears into the stacks.

Chocolate. I can do chocolate.

SEPTEMBER

It's supposed to be a standard meeting, to discuss my academic future with my supervisor, and a representative of the Basilisk Board.

Scholarship opportunities. Research networking. All that shit.

I'm fizzing, because I've nailed down my original thesis spell, and it's good. It's everything Fordyce wants and more. I can't wait to lay it out for him.

Only, he's not here. No supervisor for me. I should have known something was up, with the unexpected venue change.

Three members of the Basilisk Board are sitting around the epic troll-sized table in Meeting Room 3, waiting. Not a friendly face in sight. Professor Archibald Charmsnare the Seventh, Vice-Chancellor of the College of Real. Sorrell Merryweather. Norris Asteria.

No sign of Victor Vale or the Nightshades. Not that Viola and Jules' family members would necessarily be in my corner, before or after the New Year's Shitastrophe.

But I know for a fact that the Vales and Nightshades are no longer on Team Chauvelin. The Vice-Chancellor, the Merry-weathers and Asterias might have been nowhere in sight during the court case Jules' mum brought against Ferd's parents, but that doesn't mean they approve of her going after two of their most powerful Board members.

(The Chauvelins have not resigned from the Board despite everything. Their names still appear all over campus, though they haven't been seen in person for a while. I assumed that Belladonna U was pretending the whole thing never happened, hoping no one would notice. And that at some point in the future, there would be some quiet erasing of legacy. I guess that was too optimistic.)

There's a stink in the air, and it's not looking good for me, one of the witnesses to the Great Chauvelin Disgrace.

"Where's Professor Fordyce?" I ask, before I even sit down.

"Professor Fordyce no longer works for this university," says Professor Charmsnare, displaying none of the creepy Santa-like good humour he usually puts on for the students. He's all business. "We're here to discuss your future, Mr McClaren."

Well, fuck.

OCTOBER

> **HOLLYRULESTHEWORLD HAS OPENED THIS MIRRORCHAT**
>
> **HollyRulesTheWorld:** it can't be that hard to find a kickass venue to put on a New Year's show. We're practically famous
>
> > **SagePlaysTheDrums:** Hol. We were practically famous last year. What have we done lately
>
> **HollyRulesTheWorld:** you're the loser who decided to stay in school
>
> > **SagePlaysTheDrums:** yeah and look how far that got me
>
> **HollyRulesTheWorld:** I've seriously tried every possible venue within walking distance of campus, and nothing
>
> > **SagePlaysTheDrums:** tried going further afield?
>
> **HollyRulesTheWorld:** broomsticks are for losers
>
> > **SagePlaysTheDrums:** is it true Juniper banned you from flying for the sake of your safety and that of the people around you?

HollyRulesTheWorld: banned is a strong word

HollyRulesTheWorld: every time I'm around her
I agree with her, it's basically magic

HollyRulesTheWorld: where are u anyway we
need to strategise???

SagePlaysTheDrums: on a tram to the middle
of nowhere

HollyRulesTheWorld: wtf

HollyRulesTheWorld: why

HollyRulesTheWorld: SAGE

So, yeah, I'm basically a detective now.

I find Professor Fordyce at the Hell Broth, a pub in the outer
suburbs, with some kind of giant cow shed tacked on to the side.
There are gig posters papered everywhere, sun-faded and flutter-
ing. It looks like a scene from a dystopian movie set in a future
where live music has been banned, and can only be performed in
secret.

Was he… actually cool this whole time?

It's the middle of the day, and the heat of the summer is
already coming in. As if stepping into the bar full of day drinkers
isn't Mad Max enough for me, the bartender is a goth with spiky
hair, an equally spiky collar, and a surprising red flannel shirt
tied around her waist.

She has a tattoo of a bat on the side of her neck.

"I'm looking for Professor Fordyce," I say, remembering too
late that Professor probably isn't his first name.

The goth bartender rolls her eyes. "He's out the back, just
don't interrupt the gamers or one of them will maim you with a
dice throw."

Huh. That does look like a table of D&D going on, in the far corner by the door. And right above them, a poster advertising feminist poetry readings. I survey my surroundings more closely, and notice that three of the day drinkers by the window are wearing anime shirts and waving paperbacks at each other.

"Is this a geek bar?" I blurt out.

The bartender gazes at me, unimpressed, then points to her cocktail menu. They are all, literally all named after fictional spaceships.

Before I stop to think about it, I follow up with: "Do you have any live music booked for New Year's?"

———

It's another ten minutes before I go hunting for Fordyce. He's counting crates of craft beer, which isn't what I expected from an angry, recently-fired professor.

"So that's it?" I demand. "You're letting them run you out of academia?"

Fordyce, in a tighter black t-shirt than he ever wore around Belladonna U (and a good thing too, he was already typecast as the hot professor, a shirt this tight would have caused actual swooning in the corridors) rolls his eyes so hard that I instantly see the family resemblance. "This is my sister's bar, Sage. I'm working here until I take up my next academic job in January. In Stockholm, actually. A very prestigious university, far from here, where I get free rein over my curriculum."

"It still sucks."

"It does, but I'm hoping Nattmara Institutet isn't run by a cabal of incestuous, power-hungry warlocks with a grudge."

"It's still a uni, don't get your expectations too high."

We almost laugh at that. But… yeah, it's not funny yet. Give it a decade.

Fordyce's face softens. "Look, Sage. Keep your head down. Get your thesis submitted. There's too much oversight for them to sabotage you directly. Get your qualification and get out. The world's a big place, and the Chauvelins and Charmsnares of this world can only reach so far."

"Ha. It gets better, then."

He winces. "No. But sometimes, a few of them face consequences for doing shitty things and it almost feels worthwhile."

———

SAGEPLAYSTHEDRUMS HAS OPENED THIS MIRRORCHAT

SagePlaysTheDrums: so I found us a venue for NY

HollyRulesTheWorld: whaaaaaat

———

NOVEMBER

Prof Asteria has always been a 40 carat arsehole. He swans around campus in his tweed outfits like he belongs here, but he hasn't taught students in decades. I'm not sure what he actually does except collect rare books in his office (both his collection and his literal fucking office gets mysteriously larger each year) and vote against any progressive motion at Departmental meetings.

Oh, and one time when a gang of firsties put a petition together years ago to protest the lack of comparable resources between the Colleges of the Real and Unreal (shocker, the departments full of magic-users suck up all the money), he literally set their documentation on fire.

Asteria has officially been our supervisor — me and Liza and Dinesh — since Professor Fordyce was elbowed out 8 weeks ago. In that time, his active supervision has consisted of him putting his head in our office one time, saying "I suppose you all know what you're doing, don't mind me," and then fucking off to lunch somewhere.

———

It's thesis day. Exams are over. Classes are over. Only this remains, our final thesis spell to be presented. It's Dem Thaum Phen after all — Demonstrative Thaumaturgical Phenomena. Without our demonstration of an active piece of magic, we won't make the grade.

Liza goes up first, serving a perfectly adequate piece of spellcraft: a precise bone-detector for practical use in archaeology and modern crime forensics. It builds on some crafty theory from one of our Old Fellows right here at Belladonna U, so it's the perfect balance of modern and vintage to tick all the approval boxes.

She's a canny witch, is Liza. She saw the writing on the wall the second we lost Fordyce, and swerved her more outlandish plans for experimental archaeology hexes into something entirely conservative and practical. Safe.

Prof Asteria nods, and makes some notes as Liza completes her demonstration using a fish tank full of dirt, with strategically placed old bones inside. "Approved," he mutters, slapping down the signed form that will permit her spell to be shown to the Board, who serve as our final examiners.

Dinesh goes next. His was always bland, to be honest. Magical engineering bores the pants off me, and his little widgets for improving telekinetic construction by an eighth of a centimetre is enough to make any half-decent witch yawn.

Prof Asteria barely glances up, but approves the spell for the Board.

Now it's me. Good old, salt of the earth, born-with-the-opposite-of-a-silver-spoon-in-his-mouth Sage McClaren. Rough as guts. The warlock from the wrong side of the tracks, who talks like he's never been invited to a dinner party. Who Even Are His Parents Anyway.

Scholarship guy. Drummer. Gay.

Surprise success story.

Suspiciously high marks.

Reputation for insolence and general disrespect.

Me.

———

Slowly, I unwrap my masterpiece. It doesn't look like much. A basic porcelain jar with a very tight lid. I bought it at that shop where Hebe works now, the one full of candles and fancy throw rugs.

Not sure what this container was designed for originally. Bath bombs or pot pourri cubes or tiny rolled up hand-towels.

Today, it's full of possibility.

"I see we're going for mythic symbolism," drones Asteria, noting the flame sigil on the lid. (I got Ferd to draw it for me, he's got really into pen and ink artwork lately.)

"All the best magic has a historical footprint," I say with a wide grin.

It's a quote from a paper Prof Asteria himself published in the 70s, back when he actually bothered to contribute to the academic world. Before tenure sucked all the moisture out of his bones.

He blinks, as if he can't quite remember the person who wrote that line, but he still senses the empty flattery hanging in the air between us. "Quite, quite. And what is inside this jar of yours? Not all the evils of the world, I hope." He chuckles.

I don't.

Out of the corner of my eye I see Dinesh, who's always had a sixth sense for how to avoid trouble, quietly start to tidy up his papers, like he's prepping for a quick escape. Liza's eyes grow wider and wider. She gets me.

I explain further. "It's a complex curse based on Isadora Tallalay's Basilisk Triangle, which is itself based on Morgan Le Fey's Medea Triangle, though stabilised through a mass effect location wave charm. That's the original part."

"You —" I've never seen an old white guy go *quite* so white before. He looks like bleached paper on a sunny day at the beach. "You can't be serious."

"Deadly."

"Using one of those — after —"

Oh yeah, the Basilisk Triangle was famously used quite recently, by Ferd Chauvelin's parents, in a highly immoral attempt to restore his lost magic. Dire consequences ensued, though not as dire as they could have been — Jules and Vale were caught up in the spell, without their consent, and they *could have died*. Hebe did nearly die.

I know how serious this is.

All the media attention finally died down after Irene Nightshade's successful civil court case in May. But if a spell with this profile was set off in this university as part of the Real Honours programme, well. I imagine that interest would start up again, wouldn't it? People might start asking questions like: whatever did happen to those criminal charges that were supposed to be brought against the Chauvelins, has that court case actually been postponed three times already this year, isn't that just a bit dodgy?

"What does it do?" hisses Prof Asteria. He's no longer looking at me like I'm slime under his shoe; he's finally recognised me for the enemy I am.

"This?" I say lightly. "It's a recurring time lapse spell that will swap the magical powers of every Belladonna U student and staff member randomly for 24 hours."

"Every…" He blanches even paler. I can practically see through him. "That is an immensely destructive piece of magic, Mr McClaren."

"I filled in the ethics forms."

The thing about Dem Thaum Phen (Hons), the really funny thing about it as a subject is, there are no actual limits on what spell you submit for your final thesis. In 1958, Jules' great-grandfather straight up murdered three of his fellow students with a Hydra Sting Jinx.

They really should have fixed some of the College of the Real's more antique bylaws by now. It's still legal to hunt people of null magical abilities, if you're within ten metres of the ornamental lake.

I perfected my thesis spell three weeks ago, and since then I've spent all my time in the stacks, deep researching all the bullshit that the Department of the Real and the Basilisk Board have got away with over the years, particularly when it comes to fucking over the Department of the Unreal, and any student without high magical ability.

I've got enough on them to write a book.

Or a tell-all article for some fancy literary journal.

Or a song.

It's probably gonna be a limerick, let's be honest.

"I can't approve this spell to be tested under examination conditions," says Prof Asteria.

"I know," I say calmly.

"This subject is Demonstrative Thaumaturgical Phenomena. Unless you can submit another original spell as your thesis…"

"Nope, I'm good."

"You will not pass your Honours degree."

I lean in, just a little. "Did you know that if I quit before the end of semester, I have to pay back all my scholarship funding? But failing out — that's just bad luck."

"Please leave this room now," says the professor. "Spell *not* approved."

So I take my jar.

And I walk out of Belladonna University.

———

DECEMBER

"Sage!" Jules calls from somewhere. "What the hell are you doing?"

Good question. What am I doing?

Why am I standing in the middle of the freaking ornamental lake, on a campus where I'm no longer a student?

What the fuck am I doing?

My magic wells up inside me, wild and spiralling. Filled with all the frustrations of this past year. It would be so easy to unleash it on the world.

I'm just some bloke, standing in front of a jar full of the most dangerous spell anyone's ever devised in the history of Belladonna U.

I know exactly what I'm doing.

Some serious fucking damage.

JANUARY

Hebe breaking up with him wasn't even the worst thing that happened to Ferd that January. It didn't make the list.

Hebe saying "I don't think I'm the person you need right now" was an anti-climax, really. A sentence tacked on to the worst chapter of his life.

January was the month that Viola left.

January was the month that Jules drifted away.

January was the month that Ferd lost his family, and his childhood home.

January was the month that took his magic from him, for a second time.

January sucked balls.

———

FEBRUARY

February also sucked.

MARCH

"Do you know how many non-magical Members of Parliament we have right now, in this country?" asks Ferd's tutor in Unreal Integration Studies.

No one's hand goes up. There are twelve people in the seminar, and no one knows.

Ferd has done the reading. "Two," he says. "Both independents, not affiliated with the major parties."

"Wait," says another student. "Is that all?"

APRIL

"I have to invent some kind of spell that's never been done before, to impress my professor," said Sage.

"Sucks to be you," said Ferd. "I have to write an essay on magical privilege for a professor who literally winces every time he hears my family name."

"Sucks to be you," said Sage. "Beer?"

"Beer."

MAY

They were snapped by the paps outside the courthouse.

Sage flung an arm around Ferd's shoulders. "Smile for the cameras. Might get some publicity for the band out of this."

"Oh," said Ferd lightly. "Are you in a band?"

He doesn't know how to feel.

A judge ruled that yes, his parents were shitty enough human beings that they performed experimental, non-consensual magic on not only their son but also his two best friends.

Should he feel traumatised? Wounded? Vindicated? Right now all he felt was horrifyingly sober.

"Tell me the truth," said Sage as they headed away from the small clutch of reporters and cameras, hopefully in the direction of a pub. "How rich is Nightshade now? Should I be angling for a proposal? I could rock the trophy husband thing."

"Hate to tell you," said Ferd. "He was already horrifyingly rich. If his grandfather ever proves to be mortal, he'll own half the city."

"Fuck," said Sage. "That's distressing."

———

JUNE

"Vale."

"Chauv."

They stood awkwardly blinking at each other for a moment in the university bookshop.

Ferd broke first. "You're back. That's great. How was Paris?"

"Amazing, obviously."

With the counter between them, they couldn't exactly hug, and somehow that made it even more awkward.

"You work here now?" Vale said, glancing around.

"I have like three different student jobs. Never enough hours in just one."

"They really cut you off, then."

Even when he pulled away from them, a year and a half ago, and set out to be independent, he'd still had access to the family credit cards. Since January, nothing. Every bridge burnt.

"So much. So hard. Looking back, I really should have

prepared myself earlier for pure 100% rejection, but I never got around to it."

"That's on brand for you," Vale said, deadpan, and just like that, he had his friend back.

JULY

"Would this be your first ink?" asked the tattoo artist.

Complicated question. Ferd did his best to explain in a low-key way, but it didn't exactly come out low-key. At least his voice didn't shake as he got the story out.

"Whoa."

"Yeah."

"So it's like, entirely on your girlfriend now?"

"Ex-girlfriend."

"*Awkward.* So… do you want another phoenix this time around?"

"Definitely not."

AUGUST

> JUNIPER: so the new season of Vexington just dropped, a week early

> FERD: come on Juniper, aren't sexy costume dramas kind of over

> JUNIPER: you are my last friend who is an undergrad, are you really too busy for this?

> FERD: getting a real job turned you harsh

FERD: obviously I'm coming to watch it with you, just looking for that top hat Jules bought me last year

JUNIPER: hilarious how he thought that was a gag gift and not something you would genuinely enjoy

FERD: tough talk from a 21st century witch with a literal bonnet collection

JUNIPER: so uh, do you mind if Holly watches it with us?

FERD: is Holly secretly into sexy costume drama? Because she made a LOT of fun of us last season

JUNIPER: she has caught up on the first 2 seasons and is prepared to wear a bonnet for the occasion.

FERD: holy fuck are you two together?

JUNIPER: ...

FERD: seriously she can't join in unless she wears the bonnet.

JUNIPER: remember when you first moved in upstairs and you were less geeky?

FERD: I do not

SEPTEMBER

Tasks at a university bookshop that generally require magic for the staff to resolve safely:

- At the end of every shift, someone has to catch all the flying broomstick textbooks that have escaped the

shelves and are hovering somewhere above the staircase. That person can't be Mandrake, because of his broomstick allergy.
- Witch duels always break out in the Romance section, no way to prevent that, just accept it and move on.
- Our returns policy involves scanning books with an attuned crystal wand to find out if the spells inside have been cast since purchase in any capacity that might be considered criminal.
- Yes, Debra, you actually have to be a magic-user to operate a crystal wand.
- No, Debra, you can't fire a staff member for not being physically able to operate a crystal wand.
- Yes, Ferdinand, you may put in the complaint form about Debra's harassment of unmagical staff.

Tasks at a bar that generally require magic for the staff to resolve safely:

- Many cocktail ingredients are also potion ingredients, regardless of whether or not they have been blended with vodka.
- Our ice machine was bought off an Ice Troll family and sometimes it casts random freezing spells within a 3 metre radius.
- The AV gear for the live music acts is magical, not technological, so incompatible with almost everything else in the bar. (Thanks for that purchasing choice, Sandra!)

Tasks at a mobile phone repair help desk that require magic for the staff to resolve safely:

- Literally every job involves someone's phone reacting badly with someone's magic, and 50% of the time they're still sparking badly when they arrive and need some kind of emergency magical intervention.
- No Gary, a bucket full of salt doesn't solve everything.
- The break room is locked by password-operated hex.

OCTOBER

"Hebe. Hi."

"Ferd! You're here. At my workplace."

"I was just passing. Thought I'd pick up a... decorative pumpkin bowl. Just in time for Halloween."

"Those are for display only. I could do you a lavender candle that smells like decorative pumpkin."

"Is that better or worse than a candle that smells like actual pumpkin?"

"Opinions are divided. So, how have you been?"

"Good. Excellent. Busy."

"That's right, you must be nearly done with undergrad. How is it all going?"

"Political. Deeply — I'm doing a lot of political classes. Interesting stuff. Thinking of looking for some kind of internship next year."

"Oh, that's great. Isn't Juniper in a government job?"

"Yes, but she hates it. Besides, I was kind of hoping for..."

"The other party?"

"Literally any other party. I'd print posters for the Better Snags in Bread Party if I thought it might take any votes away from the current government."

"I thought of volunteering for BSBP, but they're not a very woman-friendly outfit."

"Really?"

"Total sausagefest."

"Ha!"

"I can't believe you didn't say it first."

"I was being cool."

"Clearly."

"Do you... want to get lunch some time?"

"That would be nice."

———

NOVEMBER

"Seriously?" said Ferd.

"Seriously," said Sage.

"You just —"

"Oh yeah." Sage mimed a spell explosion going very, very badly.

"You're not going to pass Honours?"

"The phrase you're looking for is failed. I have massively failed. Failed with extreme prejudice."

"Beer?"

"Beer."

"So, uh... where's the Destruction Jar now?"

"Top of the fridge."

"Cool, good to know."

———

DECEMBER

It's Sunday night, late. Ferd can't sleep. He taps lightly on Sage's door, eases it open in case he's interrupting.

No Sage, but Nightshade is sitting up in his rumpled bed by the light of a small, glowing illusion of a butterfly. He has an enchanted mirror resting on his knees, frowning as he reads from it.

He looks like a grown up.

"Psst," says Ferd, like he's twelve years old. "Want to get wasted?"

Jules Nightshade blinks, and then smiles a surprisingly wicked smile. "Well," he says. "It is still the weekend."

———

Neither of them have been drinking much lately, so they go down hard. Rum, Coke, watching anime while putting on fake British accents, the whole 9 yards. "Vale should be here," mutters Jules, half-focused on the blinking, bright colours of the TV.

"Maybe without the cartoons. I don't feel she'd appreciate Wizard Bikkies."

But yes. The three of them. How long has it been since three of them hung out together?

(*Maybe if you hadn't been such a shit and pushed them both away all year, because their very existence makes it hard to forget about your parents, your old life, your scary lack of a safety net to catch you when you fall...*)

Jules snickers and whacks him on the arm. "Cake Wizards. Don't let Mei hear you say that."

"Who even are you this year?" There's something else wrong with the idea of inviting Vale to join them. Ferd can't quite put his finger on it... "Thesis!" he shouts suddenly. "Her thesis. It's due soon. We should totally do this again when she's all thesised out." He glances around. "No more Coke for the rum."

"We should stop drinking?"

"Six pack of Beltaine in the fridge."

"Let's do it."

Ferd was not drunk. He could walk on his feet all the way to the kitchen. Woo. "Where's Sage, anyway? It's late."

"Don't know," sighed Jules. "He's been distracted all weekend."

"Gross."

"Not by me! I wish. Some uni bullshit, I don't know."

Ferd stared at the fridge. It still had the scorched magic mark of his hand on it, just in case he wanted to be reminded of one of the worst days of his life. "At this time of night?"

"Don't ask me. He said he was going to the campus to sort some shit out, don't wait up. He can take care of himself. Have you seen his arms?"

"Yeah, yeah, they're dreamy." Ferd looks up, to the top of the fridge. The innocuous-looking porcelain jar that has been sitting up there for several weeks is missing. *Sage is missing. Sage is at the university, sorting things out...*

Shit, he is way too drunk for this.

"Nightshade?"

"Yes, Chauvelin, old bean?"

"Don't want to freak you out, but your boyfriend might be doing something *really* stupid right now."

DECEMBER

"What do you mean, Sage is going to destroy the university?"
Viola hissed as she, Jules and Chauvelin flew slow loops around
the campus.

Chauv was on the back of Jules' broom — it always threw
her, remembering all over again that he couldn't fly without
assistance. Even though it had been years and they should be
used to it by now.

"He's been off lately," said Chauv. "Ever since all that shit
went down with his exam."

"His what?" Jules and Viola said at the same time.

"What happened with his exam?" she pressed.

"Why would he not tell me about it?" Jules demanded.

"Oh, I don't know, maybe because you've both been AWOL
lately."

"That's not fair," said Jules.

"You're his boyfriend. You should know when his life blows
up. Shouldn't you?"

"When was this?"

"Wait," said Viola. It was cold. Why was the air so cold? It was summer. High summer. "The Honours exams were weeks ago. It can't be that bad, or we would have…"

Chauv groaned. "He sparked out, okay? Destroyed his Honours final on impact. And I reckon he did it deliberately."

"Are you saying he failed?" Viola didn't want to panic. She didn't want to make this all about her. But the thought of a brilliant magic-worker like Sage flunking Honours hit her right in the most anxious part of her brain.

"Deliberately?" Jules echoed.

"He put together a spell so fucking dangerous they basically had to reject it. And there was all that shit with Professor Fordyce getting canned."

"I heard about that," said Viola. "Everyone in my department was talking about it. I talked to Sage about what was going on, back in *October*, I haven't been completely out of the loop."

"I think I have," said Jules, looking sick. "He never mentioned any of this to me at all."

"He said he could handle it," Viola said stubbornly.

"He handled it, all right," said Chauv. "Handled it completely — ugh. Brain so foggy."

"I could sober you up," said Viola. "Unlike the two of you I didn't feel the need to swallow the entire contents of a bar before kicking off a mercy dash."

"No, it's fine. Cold air is doing the trick. I don't know if I want to be all the way sober for this."

"We should bring more people," said Jules. "Like. His actual friends."

"Shut up, we're his friends," said Viola. "Also, I see him. Down there! Tell me fast, exactly what kind of spell did he serve up to the examiners?"

———

Sage was a dark silhouette in front of the oddly bright lake, glittering with pale stars. She could feel his magic as they approached, like the warmth given off by a bonfire.

"Sage," called Jules. "What the hell are you doing?"

"Tactful," said Viola.

Sage turned around, and he wasn't just a dark shape any more. His eyes were blazing with magic. Fire. Colour. Fury.

"I'm texting Hebe," Chauv said in an undertone.

"We should have brought so much coffee," whispered Jules.

"Sage," said Viola. "Turn off the psycho meltdown for a minute. I want to talk to you."

"You're supposed to be the diplomatic one," Jules sputtered.

"I am *very* tired," she said back.

"Vale," said Sage. He sounded tired too. "Did I tell you about my jar?"

"Sage," Viola snarled. "Tell me that you're not all fired up to use the same stupid spell on the whole student populace that so thoroughly fucked up a very small group of us a year ago."

"I fixed it," he said. "It definitely wouldn't kill people. Just give everyone a taste of how the other half lives. You wouldn't understand."

"Oh, and it's only going to hurt the Basilisks, is it? The ones most complicit in the fucked up class system at this university? Or is it going to wreck everyone? You think if some null firstie who's never cast a Light Up charm before ends up saddled with your messy powerhouse of magic casting ability, it won't cause some kind of house fire catastrophe?"

Sage shook his head and stepped backwards, up to his ankles in lake water. "Don't worry about it. It won't affect you. You're not even staying, right?"

Viola opened her mouth to yell at him, because that was a secret, she hadn't even made her mind up about Paris yet...

Sage was already turning away. The glittering waters of the lake rose up around him, like a sphere of protection, closing him off from her.

Whatever it was he wanted to do to this place, she'd blown her chance to talk him out of it.

———

"What now?" demanded Chauv.

"I don't know," Viola said back, infuriated. "Wait and find out what kind of damage he has in mind, I guess."

The three of them stood there, stunned and wretched. Waiting.

"So," said Chauv. "How's everyone else's year going?"

Jules staggered a few steps away from them and threw up messily into a hedge. "I'm a spy," he blurted out when he came up for air. "I work for the — it's not hex development, not private surveillance. I work for the government in Real Intelligence, I'm a fucking spy. And the pay is *shit*."

Viola stared at him.

Chauv stared at him.

For once in her life, Viola had absolutely no idea what to say.

But when she started laughing maniacally, with no way of stopping, Chauv joined in.

CHAPTER TEN
THE YEAR OF HEBE

JANUARY

I broke up with Ferd on a Thursday.

Technically we weren't back together yet.

Technically he broke up with me the previous month, while under the influence of a magical house's stolen power. Technically, he never meant to do that.

Technically...

There's only so far a relationship can go on a technicality.

I said "don't overthink it" at the time, but ever since we sort of maybe got back together, I've been doing nothing but think.

Since his parents were arrested.

Since I nearly died.

Since Ferdinand Chauvelin's old magic tattoo transferred itself to my shoulder, without my consent.

We had the occasional coffee together, awkward and sweet.

We started a whole bunch of conversations that went nowhere.

And then.

And then.

———

I broke up with Ferd on a Thursday. It seemed like a good idea at the time.

He had Viola and Jules, after all. The three of them had been clinging to each other like limpets since all that business on New Year's Day.

I had my own things to think about. A future that didn't make sense to me, not yet.

———

A week earlier, on the Thursday before I broke up with Ferd, I broke up with Belladonna University. And that… that was the thing that nearly broke me.

It wasn't that I had been a student for so long. (My whole life, basically.) Walking away from the Department of the Unreal for the last time, I had a bit of a revelation. I had been a *good* student for so long. Being a good student was part of my identity. It was my identity.

Hebe Hallow got great marks. Teachers and professors liked her. She got her assignments in on time. This was who she was.

Who was I, without her?

———

"I get it," said Ferd, stirring his coffee slowly.

"Do you, though?" I was so far inside my head, I didn't realise what I was saying until I said it.

His face changed; became incredulous. "Yes, actually I do understand what it's like to have your whole identity revolve around being good at school, and have that ripped away."

"Sorry," I said, startled. Of course he did. He'd been spiralling around recovery from his loss of identity for as long as I had known him.

"I get the other thing, too," he said, more gently. "Wanting to keep your distance. I'd run a mile from all my family bullshit if I could. I don't blame you."

Somehow, that made it worse.

"I'm not going anywhere," I said, because I didn't know yet I was going to break up with him, one week later.

"Do whatever you need to do," he said, standing up, heading to the counter, to pay our bill. "*I get it,* Hebe. Don't worry about it."

It was as if this was what he had always expected, from our relationship.

From me.

———

FEBRUARY

On a Monday, I went to each of my student jobs, and handed in my notice.

Gloria at the Desiree O'Dowd Unreal Library said:

> *We could keep you on with reduced hours if you need more time to do your Magical Archivist Diploma. Or you can switch to one of the Real Libraries if that would be more useful for your vocational experience. We'll give you a great reference.*

(I didn't want to tell her that I had given up on the Magical Archivist Diploma too. She was so proud when they accepted me.)

Henny at the student advice desk said:

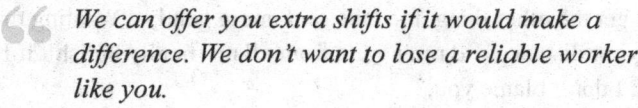

We can offer you extra shifts if it would make a difference. We don't want to lose a reliable worker like you.

Mandrake at the bookshop said:

You don't even have to be a student to work here. Are you sure we can't offer you a two dollar an hour raise?

I said:

I just need to be off campus for a while. Sorry. I'll work out my notice. Whatever you need.

One by one, I cut the strings, until there was nothing tying me to Belladonna U. To this suburb. To this city.

Nothing but my home, my sister, the people I loved.

––––––

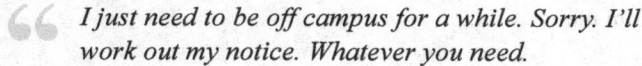

University is over. Real life starts here.

––––––

Throw cushions have always been my greatest weakness, a symbol of my embarrassingly domestic magic. I sense the presence of these particular throw cushions from three blocks away.

"Check it out," says Dec, looking way too smug. "I've gone mainstream."

Last time I saw his art on display it was in a grimy hipster warehouse exhibition. Now, it's in the window of a homewares store.

A really nice homewares store.

"Let me introduce you to Aurora," says Dec.

Part of me wants to resist, because I don't want someone else solving my problems for me. This is the year I become a proper adult. This is the year I think for myself. Life after Belladonna U.

But it's a really nice store, and it makes my magic hum.

———

When Aurora offers me a job, I say: "yes."

When she mentions there's a flat upstairs I could rent very cheaply, I say: "yes."

And just like that, my new life begins.

———

MARCH

Holly seems fine about me moving out. Almost too fine. She's busy with her corporate music job and barely seems to notice.

Mei is kind, but judgy, which is par for the course with Mei.

It's Sage and Dec who help me move my stuff into the new flat which is tiny but already super cozy.

"Why does this place smell like roses?" asks Dec. "And... happiness?"

"Thanks for doing this," I say again, on the second trip up the narrow staircase, all of our arms filled with boxes.

"No worries," says Sage. "What am I going to do instead, go to band practice?" He scoffs, as if the absurdity of that might need to be pointed out. The band has disappeared, basically. Since the summer.

"Has anyone heard from Juniper?" I should have checked in on her by now. I keep meaning to text. She's been in Tasmania longer than anyone expected.

"Hey," says Sage at one point, catching my arm. "I know

you're doing this whole independence thing right now. But you'll come to this game Mei's set up, won't you?"

"Sure, of course. Cake Wizards. It will be fun."

I haven't even managed to watch a single episode of Cake Wizards yet.

But I can't lose track of my friends.

Fannish gaming shenanigans are exactly the best way for us to stay in touch. No pressure.

———

APRIL

This month's excuses for not turning up to the Cake Wizards game:

- Working a late shift on a Saturday
- Working an early shift on Sunday (can't stay up late)
- Bit of a cold
- It's just been a really long week.

———

HOLLYRULESTHE WORLD HAS OPENED THIS
MIRRORCHAT

HollyRulesTheWorld: so Juniper's home

> HebeIsSoBoring: awesome. Are you going to
> start practice again soon, look for a new venue
> for regular gigs?

HollyRulesTheWorld: maybe, plans for a new
album. Excitement!

HollyRulesTheWorld: Juniper's renting your
room, are you OK with that?

HollyRulesTheWorld: also I quit my job

HebeIsSoBoring: omg what happened?

HollyRulesTheWorld: you know, life!changing! revelations, that sort of thing

HollyRulesTheWorld: wanna get lunch?

HebeIsSoBoring: sure, of course

———

MAY

I should text Ferd. Ex or no ex, you don't let a month go by when a friend's parents are in the middle of a massive life-changing court case (that involves your own testimony) without at least texting.

I don't text.

Instead, I mainline every episode of Cake Wizards.

They're right. It's a super cute, escapist anime. I'm definitely going to write fanfic.

I could message Mei, suggest I slot into the game now I've done my homework.

But I don't.

———

HEBE: hey

DEC: hey

HEBE: want to come over?

DEC: [thumbs up]

———

JUNE

My magic is calm. I haven't created bonus throw cushions in six weeks. I haven't needed to, not with the homewares in Aurora's shop all singing my praises, making my domestic magic feel happy and wanted and at home.

There's a new range of thistledown quilts, and we're nearly sold out.

I really, really like my job.

————

"Are you sure you don't want something more challenging?" Mum asks on one of my calls home.

The mums were supportive of my new job, of my choice to leave uni (or as they put it "to take a break from academia"), but they're starting to get restless now the year is half over and I'm still working retail. I'm not sure exactly what they expected.

"Not everything has to be challenging," I tell them. "I'm doing well. I'm happy."

"Well."

"Of course we want you to be happy!"

"Can you put Holly on the phone?"

"She's not here," I sigh. "We don't live together any more, remember?"

"Oh, of course. But you still see each other. Don't you?"

"Not as much as we probably should. It's okay, Mum. Everything's okay."

————

JULY

HEBE HAS OPENED THIS MIRRORCHAT

Hebe: How are you doing, how's Honours going?

SagePlaysThe Drums: All good. How's the job going?

Hebe: All good.

———

HEBE: are you free this Friday

DEC: I have to prowl around a bunch of museums getting inspiration for a new commission

DEC: wanna join me?

HEBE: always

———

AUGUST

Seeing Viola was just so weird.

I thought I was keeping up with people. I texted, and sent memes. I MirrorChatted. Sometimes there was meeting for coffee, or meeting for lunch.

This is how grown ups do socialising, I told myself. You don't have to all live in some kind of magical share house arrangement to enjoy each other's company. You're not eighteen anymore.

But seeing Viola was like pulling a cloth away and realising how much time had passed. She went to France for half a year. Holly changed jobs. Sage is... actually I'm not sure how Sage is doing. How much do I suck?

I've been staying away, because I feel weird about

Belladonna U, not my friends. Unfortunately, most of my friends still live, work and party within three blocks of the campus.

It's just a place. It disappointed me a little, towards the end, and I disappointed it right back. It didn't actually try to murder me, like another house I might mention.

It's just uni. I can handle it.

Right?

————

So it's my day off and I'm totally going to wander in the direction of the Manic Pixie Dream House. I even get off one tram stop early, to prove I'm not trying to avoid the campus itself.

It's a weekday. Students everywhere. They all look so young.

I'm barely into my twenties. Why do those kids all look so young?

————

I make my way quickly past the bookshop (so weird to walk past a bookshop without plastering myself to the window and immediately going inside) and the Fennysnake Cafe (best unhealthy breakfast in the area).

And there it is, finally. A mostly sturdy two storey house with some odd paint choices (pink and green!) and a garage much larger than any other on the street.

The garage door is open, which means Dec, at least, is home. Dec's easy. I have no unresolved guilt issues around Dec.

I mean, we probably shouldn't be having casual sex as much as we have been over the last few months, but that's more of a 'you're putting off real life choices' mistake than an actual 'this will wreck your life' mistake.

The smell of dye chemicals hits me smack in the face. Is it

healthy for him to breathe in all that stuff? Probably not.

"Hello?"

"Hebes!" Dec emerges from his art cave, clay-smeared and cheerful. "Look at you, I thought you'd forgotten this side of the city existed."

Oh, he's hot. That's random and unfair.

"Axe," I manage to say, because he's holding a truly terrifying vintage and/or replica weapon.

"Oh." Dec blinks in the sunlight as if realising for the first time that he's armed. "Hang on." He and the axe disappear back into the miasma of fumes.

"Are the ice trolls getting feisty on the streets again?" I call after him. "Or is this a cosplay thing?"

"Nah. It's just a prop for my queen-in-progress. Obviously." He emerges again, wiping his hands on a reasonably clean cloth before opening his arms wide for a hug.

Even hugging him is uncomplicated.

"Have you found a model yet, for your Clytemnestra?"

"Nah."

We tried it out — I've modelled for him before. But I could tell it wasn't working. I can't pull off imperious fury, and no one wants to be an artist's pity muse.

Viola would be perfect, obviously, but Viola has a PhD thesis burning her brain, and besides, I'm pretty sure she and Dec aren't on speaking terms.

"Is anyone else home?" I ask. "I was hoping to catch up with people. You know. Everybody."

"This time of day? Nah." Dec wipes what looked like a piece of clay from his hair. "Mei is Broomdashing way more hours than is strictly legal, to save up for her big trip. Sage and Ferd are at uni, Juniper's at work. Holly's at work. Jules is… well, you get the idea. Working people."

"Does Jules live here now?" I want to ask more questions, about this trip Mei is planning (since when?), about where Holly is even working now, but that isn't fair. I see Dec more than any of the rest of them. He shouldn't have to be my conduit.

I need to make more time for my people. I need to want to hang out, just because. The year has been rattling by so fast...

"Depends on the week. He's here more than Sage, sometimes." Dec gives me a thoughtful, searing look that kind of makes me wonder what underwear I put on this morning. "What do you really want to know?"

I don't know where to start.

"Nothing really. I guess I should leave you to it."

"Nah, I can take a break." He gives me a slow, lazy look. This, at least, I recognise. "Could do with a shower and a beer in that order. Want to join?"

Well, it's not like I have to to be anywhere...

SEPTEMBER

Sometimes at night I think I can hear its wings flapping. Which is not what you want in a tattoo.

I've been trying not to think about it, how I was marked by that whole business with the house and Ferd's parents.

His magic. Its absence was a part of our relationship, in a way. We'd never have met and become so close if he wasn't forced out of his fancy Basilisk life. Jules and Viola wouldn't be all tangled up with my friends.

And then, after all that... a phoenix, living on my skin. I can't give it back in a box full of random items, like you normally do at the end of a relationship (I imagine — my only previous break up was with Sage and he still has half my high school music collection in a shoe box under his bed).

A little while ago, I consulted a healer about whether I could remove my uninvited tattoo, but she said I need to consider why the tattoo was there, and what it was saying to me.

If I wanted to think *that* hard about it, I'd have made an appointment with a therapist, not a skin healer.

Possibly I need to see a therapist.

I still wake up several times a night, because I'm dreaming of that house. The house that tried to kill me.

———

I don't make an appointment with a therapist. It's fine. I can just ignore the giant inked phoenix on my skin that's trying to tell me something.

———

It's possible I should talk to my friends about how I'm feeling. Talk to my sister. Holly wouldn't be bothered about a random magical tattoo exchange. She'd probably cut windows in all her clothes to show it off.

———

One night, when I woke up with a scream in my tiny, cozy apartment, alone in the middle of the city…

I thought, what would Holly do?

Then I put the light on and started writing lyrics for a song.

———

OCTOBER

> HEBE: I think maybe we should stop hooking up

> DEC: cool

> DEC: we can still hang out sometimes, yeah?

HEBE: obviously

> DEC: do you know any super angry women with axe-holding skills who could sit for me? This Clytemnestra piece is driving me up the wall

HEBE: yes I can tell you're heartbroken

NOVEMBER

The counsellor nods, looking sympathetic. A good skill if you can manage it. I'd be rubbish as a therapist. I used up all my sympathy for people at the Belladonna U help desk... a job I quit ten months ago.

I think of myself as a nice person, but how can that be true when you have to physically restrain yourself from rolling your eyes all the time?

"And how do you feel about the phoenix tattoo?" the counsellor asks.

I should have guessed this question was coming.

"I don't know."

"That's a good start."

"Is that sarcasm?"

She raises her eyebrows at me. "Do you tend to assume people are being sarcastic when they're trying to help you?"

Huh. Good point.

"How can it be good that I don't know?"

"It gives us a starting point."

"Why don't you just tell me how I'm supposed to feel?"

She smiles a little. "Let me guess. You got very good marks in school."

"You can tell that from looking at me?"

"I can tell, because you're approaching therapy like there's a way to get top marks if you give me the right answers."

Ah. That's fair.

"…is there a way to get top marks?"

DECEMBER

> FERD: Are you up?

>> HEBE: I shouldn't be. I hardly got any sleep last night because I finally made it to to a Cake Wizards session and it was epic, but I'm running on like 3 hours sleep for the whole weekend, plus I have a double shift tomorrow. What's going on? Hi. I haven't heard from you in a while.

> FERD: We need your help with Sage

>> HEBE: Is he OK?

> FERD: very much no

>> HEBE: I'll be right there

FERD

It only takes one conversation, to talk Sage off his ledge.

The trick, of course, was that it couldn't be a conversation with any of us.

It had to be Hebe.

She arrives all in a rush, a silhouette on a broomstick. It's a new broom, I notice, sleeker than the old one she used in her student days, with a few cute baubles strung over the bristles. Fashionable.

As she approaches us — me, Nightshade and Vale, standing awkwardly at the edge of the ornamental lake — a plate of ginger biscuits appear in her hands, which means she's nervous, or possibly just breathing in and out.

Her magic likes everyone to make themselves comfortable. It's not weird.

She shoves the plate at me, barely looking at any of us, and wades directly into the water, heading for Sage and his imminent nervous breakdown.

I used to feel weird about their friendship, in the early days. It's a tough thing to swallow, knowing your girlfriend has an ex in her life who would stand in front of a death-hex for her. Fight an ice troll. Throw himself off a custard cavern into jellybean territory. All the great sacrifice moves.

(I have been watching way too much Cake Wizards tonight, can you tell? Also, still drunk)

Anyway, I got over myself. Sage has been a good housemate. A good mate, full stop.

Also, he'd stand in front of a death-hex for any of his friends. Maybe even me.

————

SAGE

I can see it so clearly. How the spell would unfold. The random element. One cosmic dice throw of fuckery.

Maybe my heat and power would end up in some null librarian, or a Basilisk king I hate, or Archibald bloody Charmsnare III.

Maybe Vale would end up with no magic, or Liza's bone magic, or Hebe's throw cushion magic…

No, not Hebe's magic. She's safe. Hebe doesn't go here any more.

Maybe, if I've got this right, the entire fabric of Belladonna U would hover in a single, perfect magical moment, in which everyone has all the magic and no magic, all at once.

Maybe I should have got some fucking sleep recently.

Maybe I just want it all to burn.

"Sage," says a voice, and it's her. My Hebe. Her presence feels like a cozy blanket and a bowl of soup and a long lie-in on a Sunday.

"Hebe," I say, choking a little on her name. "Make it stop."

————

HEBE

There's something wrong with Sage.

No, like, really wrong.

I've known him for what feels like most of my life. He's one of my favourite people.

Sometimes he feels like more a part of me than my twin. I know his voice. His stupid jokes. His physical presence.

How long has this been going on? How long is it since I saw him, let alone really looked at him? Because I would have known, wouldn't I, before it got this far?

There's something in his bones that doesn't belong to him. Not fire. Not ice. An entirely new kind of magic.

It's eating him alive.

JULES

Sage is the best thing that happened to me this year.

We haven't always been at 100% for each other.

He's been distant.

I've been absent.

But when we're in sync, it's so bloody good.

Sometimes it's just both being tired and worn out and pissed off at the world at the same time, and taking comfort in each other's presence.

And I didn't know. Didn't see what was happening. Hebe fucking Hallow took one look at him, and she saw it.

I'm supposed to be observant for a living.

I think I'm going to be sick again.

VIOLA

Hebe is standing close to Sage. Too close, to be safe. If this thing is as dangerous as she thinks then…

She puts her arms around him, hugging him fiercely, as if somehow her perfect friendship connection will heal whatever horrifying magic threat has wormed its way into his body.

Demon possession?

Whatever it is, it caused him to fail his exams, and that is not okay.

Sage bursts into flames.

Jules stifles a cry, and Chauvelin holds him back.

Hebe keeps hugging Sage. The flames turn green, then purple.

The waters of the ornamental lake rise up, transforming into some kind of pale blanket that wraps itself around Sage and Hebe, dousing the flame.

No, I spoke too soon. Now the lake itself is on fire around them. Not a natural flame. It's blue, and smells like death.

Sage cries out, screams. His head is thrown back, out of the safety of the blanket. White smoke, or steam, pours from his eyes. A terrifying, seething vapour.

And then, as I stand uselessly on the side of the lake with my two best friends, we see a black shape tear away from Hebe, coming up out of the flames and the smoke. A very familiar shape. It's a phoenix, made of ink.

I always told Chauv it was a pretentious choice. I guess I'm eating my words.

The phoenix wraps itself around the bone-white vapour, containing it in a black ball of caged magic. The flames die out.

Hebe reaches one hand out, towards the hovering ball of magic wrapped in magic, that used to be a phoenix tattoo, and something sinister inside our friend.

As she connects with the ball of magic, it transforms itself…

Into a throw cushion.

SAGE

"Liza," says Prof Fordyce, shaking his head. He's in another one of those too-tight black t-shirts, pouring drinks for my mates like he's been doing it all his life. I hope the students of Nattmara Institutet are prepared for this level of Aussie hot professor. "I can't believe it," he mutters.

"Yep," I say grimly. "Ancient bone curse. Local cops tracked it back to the source, a book in a protected collection at Belladonna U that only one student had borrowed in the last 25 years."

"I mean," says Fordyce, making a Manhattan Moya with his eyes practically closed. "One in ten postgrad students do try to magically sabotage their peers, but I only had three under my wing this year. I thought we'd beat the odds."

"Turns out she was banking on a postgrad fellowship for archaeology magic, and they only consider students who are dux of their year. She saw me as a threat."

"Sucks to be you," says Dinesh cheerfully, appearing at my elbow. "Doesn't pay to be top, McClaren. I've been coasting on a Distinction average since first year and no one's ever

cursed me. Beer please, professor. Whatever you've got on
tap."

"It's students like you make it all worthwhile, Dinesh," sighs
Fordyce, but he pours the beer. "Anything for you, Sage?"

The Hell Broth is jumping. Everyone's here — students,
geeks, fans of the band, random starship cocktail enthusiasts.

Holly and Juniper are on stage already, making final checks
for our epic New Year's concert. The Fake Geek Girl comeback
tour is about to begin.

"Bottle of water, thanks. The good stuff. Ice troll approved."

Fordyce grabs it for me from the fridge. "Is this band of
yours decent?"

I grin at him. "Indecent, I hope. But we rock, if that's what
you're asking."

————

VIOLA

Viola couldn't quite believe she was out in public. That recre-
ation was allowed. That she had — for the moment — literally
nothing better to do.

Nursing a Rosemary Enterprise, she found herself standing
near the side of the stage when the band took a break, and Sage
bounded off the steps to stand in front of her, sweaty and gross
in *her favourite Vixen t-shirt*, swallowing the dregs of a bottle of
water.

This at least was normal. He displayed none of the seven
standard signs that your friend is under a magical curse.

"Vale," he said when he came up for air.

"McClaren."

"Enjoy our set?"

She shook her head. "You actually did it. You wrote a whole
song about the Pandora myth and the terrible class politics at our
university."

He beamed at her. Typical Sage. When in doubt, write a song about it. "I really did. What'd you think?"

"Obviously I have notes."

"Obviously."

"Are they going to let you retake your exam? Since you were under the influence of a curse."

"Yeah," he said with a shrug, walking through the crowd towards the source of more water. "Not sure if I can be arsed."

"That's just stupid, Sage," she said, hurrying after him. She had to stay close or the crowd that was easily parting for his confident body mass would put a wall between them. "You did all the work."

"And who gets the credit if I do well? Fucking Asteria." He made it out of the music shed, all the way around to the bar, and laid his head on the surface.

An unbelievably cool-looking bartender in a tiny raven-print dress and giant black boots put a whole jug of water in front of him without him having to ask. Sage looked like he wanted to stick his entire head in it, but couldn't quite figure out the logistics.

Viola took advantage of his heat exhaustion. "This is your future, Sage," she pressed. "You could do anything. Be anything."

"Vale," he said tiredly. "I have half an hour before I go back on stage. Right now, I want to make out with my boyfriend and think about nothing."

———

JULES & JUNIPER

"Great set. Killer outfit."

"Thank you! Holly picked it out for me. Well, she picked something else but I refused to go out in public in that, and we negotiated for three hours, and then I picked my own outfit and she said I looked great."

"You always look great, darling. Will you come say hi to my mother? She wants you to sign a CD for her."

"Your mother came to the show?"

"Sure, she's been a fan ever since she found out your cello shares her first name. Did her research on YouTube and everything."

"So she's not following the band because you're dating the drummer?"

"Saving *that* fun fact for later this evening."

———

HEBE & HOLLY

"There you are!"

"Here I am!"

"Fave song?"

"All of yours, obviously."

"Shut up, for real."

"Okay. Sage's new one is great but feels faintly libellous. And I have a soft spot for Untitled Cryptid Song, obviously…"

"Obviously."

"But I like Juniper's new one, about all the sex scenes in Vexington."

"What makes you think Juniper wrote it? I sang the song!"

"Come on. There's no way you know the difference between the Countess Palatine and her three sisters…"

"You mean the hot redhead, the one who wears wallpaper print fabric, and the one who really knows how to ride a horse?"

"OMG. Holly. Are you…"

"Shut up, don't say it."

"Are you a *fangirl*?"

DEC & VIOLA

"Hey, Vi. Great dress."

"Thanks."

"Got your results yet?"

"Not for another six weeks, but thanks so much for being the twelfth person to ask me tonight, it's making the party super fun."

"Look, I know this is… But can I draw you?"

"Really? Do you not have enough sketches from the entire time we dated?"

"I'm doing *Clytemnestra*, Vi. I need a super angry model prepared to hold an axe for hours on end. No one does longterm contained fury better than you."

"Sweet, but I have a lot on right now. Fellowship applications. Family events. Holding myself back from jumping on a plane to Paris."

"I get it. No worries."

"Ask me again in February. If you can't find anyone else. And if I'm still in the country. Which I probably won't be. Did I mention Paris?"

"It's chill, Vi. All I need is a really angry woman to draw. I'm sure there's another one in this city."

"Or you could just find an ordinary woman and convince her to join your friends group. She'll be infuriated in no time."

"You love us really."

"I… might not hate you."

FERD & HEBE

"So."

"So."

"Apparently, my phoenix tattoo was a protection charm."

"Don't you mean my phoenix tattoo?"

"Ha, yes. I guess so. Is it really gone?"

"You'll have to take my word for it."

"Oh — yes. I wasn't meaning to — uh. Demand visitation rights or anything. I believe you."

"Changing the subject! How's your year been going?"

"Basically a lot like this conversation."

"Awkward and unresolved?"

"Missing you."

"Oh."

"Yeah."

———

JULES & DEC

"Nightshade. Tell me about the woman you brought."

"Please tell me you don't mean my mother."

"Nah, the other one. The tiny angry ball of fury who is currently showing that bartender how his standards for a dirty martini aren't high enough. She's outstanding."

"Her name is Serenity, she's my work partner, *please* don't get a crush on her. Our lives are incestuous enough."

"Do you think maybe she'd model for me, though?"

"I think she'd destroy you."

"Even better."

———

HEBE & FERD

"I wrote a song."

"Wait, what?"

"I was thinking about a lot of things, processing, you know. And I ended up writing a song about everything that's happened lately — this year, the things I'm trying to change about myself, the things I miss, the things I left behind. Throw cushions."

"Okay."

"It was supposed to be about me, but it kept coming back to, well. You."

"Can I hear it?"

"Nooooo, no one can hear it, I literally set fire to it so Holly would never find it and sing it in front of an audience. I would rather die."

"Right."

"But I wanted you to know. That I wrote it."

———

HEBE & MEI

"So you're just—"

"Yep."

"But that's HUGE. How can you drop everything and run off to the other side of the planet?"

"You ran off to the other side of the city, months ago."

"That's not fair."

"I'm not sniping. You did. And that's fine. You had to… be your true Hebe, or whatever. Spread your wings. Live your life. It was good for you. You seem happy."

"I came back. I am back. You're really going to Paris to share an apartment with Viola? I didn't know you two were even friends."

"I guess we'll find out."

"What are you going to do over there?"

"Write fanfic. Learn a new language. Eat croissants. My parents said they'd cover my flight costs and one month of accommodation if I got a job to support myself in Paris — and

Viola hooked me up with something through the university, tutoring in Basic Spellcasting and English language. Anyway, it might not happen. If Viola's thesis gets sent back with 'must try harder' I won't be able to afford the rent on the tiny garret apartment on my own."

"So, you picked France randomly?"

"Not randomly. If I knew someone looking for a roommate in Berlin or Mexico I'd have picked that. Though I will admit, I rolled a die to make the final decision."

"Of course you did."

"Can't argue with a critical hit."

"No, you cannot."

[pause]

"Good thing you didn't let Jules roll that die for you."

"*OMG, so true.*"

HOLLY & JUNIPER

"So, this is it. A new year."

"We were great tonight. I mean you were — you were amazing. But also *we* were amazing. I think we can really do this, Junie. Take it to the next level. Get back into crowdfunding. Build on our social media following. Are there any new social media things around?"

"There's Witchle."

"Isn't that just some game for nerds?"

"We're a *band* for nerds, Holly. Anyway, it's fun. A word puzzle where you try to figure out the spell based on guessing ingredients. There are forums, and I've seen a few artists using it to raise their profile, build conversations."

"Huh. Well, we can look into that. One way or another, this is going to be the year of Fake Geek Girl."

"I'm in if you are."

"And uh, even if you weren't. That would be okay too. I'd want to be with you even if we didn't have the band."

"That's nice to hear."

"We just have to make sure Sage doesn't waste his time getting a real job."

"Drummers have to eat."

"He can write us hit songs and *then* he can eat. What do you want, Junie?"

"Oh, no more drinks for me. I'm done for the night."

"No, I mean, what do you want? It's a new year. New possibilities. Future stuff."

"Well, we might need a new flatmate."

"Damn, that's right. Do you know anyone?"

"I thought we could ask Jules. I don't think he and Sage are quite at — you know, living together levels. But it would be convenient for him to be nearby."

"Brilliant. He can pay rent and hardly ever be home. You're an evil genius."

"And maybe… I could move out of my room? Or we could keep it for band stuff, and share the other one…"

"GENIUS FOR GOOD AND EVIL."

"And I want a cat. I wasn't allowed one at home, and then I lived in halls, and…"

"Say no more. I will buy you a dozen cats. A thousand cats."

"One small rescue cat please."

"Nope, too late to back down. The future is you and me and a cauldron full of cats."

"Maybe a small cauldron."

"There's Hebe! We have to drag her home for an afterparty."

"Did we tell anyone else there was going to be an afterparty at our house?"

"I assumed they'd just know."

———

CAKE WIZARDS

"I should be going home…"

"Hebe, no! It's early…"

"It's 3am, everyone's exhausted. You can't seriously be thinking of starting a game now."

"A little game. A teensy, tiny game."

"I suppose we could roll up a few characters."

"Jules, don't encourage them."

"Wait, does this mean we get to watch Jules roll dice? Hebes, you have to see this."

"You said that last time and he rolled a 20, so…"

"Oh, that's never happening again."

"You're not funny."

"Mei, you are leaving the country. How are you going to GM from Paris?"

"I'll find a way."

"Why do I sense sleeplessness in our future?"

"Mei laughs in the face of international time zones."

"Hebe! Roll a character."

"Okay, is this Cake Wizards still? Because I was thinking I could be one of Juniper's Creme Pat Cats…"

"No, this is something else! Ferd, you do the pitch."

"Hang on, I need my top hat for this."

"Wait, no. You have Chauv playing now? He was the last sane one!"

"Sure, Aerie Berry, dark queen of sponge."

"I only answer to Medusa these days."

"Here he comes, Lord Muck in his top hat."

"Darling fiends and gentlefriends, let me introduce you to — Vexington Manor: the Game."

"*No.*"

"Sexy Vexington? Are we getting into porno games now? I'm not complaining…"

"Much like the popular costume drama TV show, Vexington

Manor is a game of charm, wit, arranged marriages, scandalous trysts and occasional inconvenient murders. But unlike the weirdly null universe of the distressingly attractive Vexington family — this world has magic."

"Yay!"

"Boo."

"Roll your characters! Will you be a butler with butterfly wings? A devilish debutante? A matchmaking mamma using hexes and charms to score a high-ranking son-in-law?"

"Juniper, I love you, but I really don't have to be here for this."

"Holly! It will be fun. You love Vexington."

"I mean, you don't have to tell everyone…"

"You literally wrote a song about it."

"I told everyone you wrote it!"

"But there's a twist! Over to you, Dec."

"I will insist on wearing your top hat. Thank you, good sir. The twist is, everyone rolls one D20 to find their starting social rank before they design their characters. Highest scoring roll means — duke, queen, that sort of thing. Lowest is like, scullery maid or boot boy. And I think we all know who we want to roll first."

"Ah, so this whole thing is designed for my humiliation."

"Go on, Nightshade. Brave heart."

"Fine, I shall wear my scullery maid apron with pride. Here we go."

(the sound of rolling dice)

(rolling, rolling)

(stops)

(general explosion of hilarity)

LIKE WITCHES FOR COFFEE

CHAPTER ONE
FAKE GEEK GIRL VS THE PURPLE COUCH OF SIRENITY

> "They've had an amazing six months with their new album Like Witches for Coffee raising over ten times their goal on Witchstarter, and their single Coffee is the Key To Surviving You tipped to be the indie hit of the year. Let's welcome to Sirenity the band-members of Fake Geek Girl: it's Holly, Juniper and Sage!"

They crowd on to the well-loved purple guest couch, looking giddy and half-embarrassed. Holly's hair is fierce purple, in her classic spiky ponytail. Sage's shoulders seem to have expanded under studio lights. He's wearing his own band-shirt shame-lessly, a size too small. Juniper is wearing a long floaty skirt made of silk scarves, and she has a little twist of purple in her own hair, matching Holly's.

They're adorable, or at least Danika the host seems to think so. She leans in like she wants to eat them all alive.

"Let's start with that song. Coffee is the Key to Surviving You has been a massive hit. Sage, is it true you wrote it for your boyfriend?"

The drummer looks faintly embarrassed; hell of a way for

this many of their fans to find out all at once that he has a sprinkling of freckles that are only visible when he blushes. "Rumour has it."

"Why don't you sing the track?" Danika presses. "You've performed it live, but you gave it to Holly for the album?"

"She's our lead singer," says Sage quickly.

"He gets all emotional," said Holly, cheerfully throwing him under the bus. "Can't sing it without bursting into tears."

"You're the worst!" he groans. "That's a lie, Danika. Please tell your international streaming audience that Holly Hallow is a liar."

"My Love is a Cake Wizard is about his boyfriend too," chirps Holly.

Juniper scoffs.

"Better not let your girlfriend hear you say that," snarks Sage.

Two minutes later, Danika has lost control of the interview, and Sage and Holly are hitting each other with purple couch cushions.

The interview goes viral.

CHAPTER TWO
FAKE GEEK GIRL VS THE DRAGONATOR

Static bleeds into vision, the customary opening of popular music-tuber The Dragonator: a twenty-eight year old who literally films his show in a basement.

THIS WEEK: FEATURING FAKE GEEK GIRL!

Holly and Juniper are still wearing their matching purple hair. Sage is wearing a t-shirt that declares Holly Hallow is a Liar. You can buy it from the Fake Geek Girl merch store.

DRAGONATOR: Most popular question from our viewers poll — why is this album is less geeky than your earlier work, and did you screw over your longtime fans to sell out for mainstream success?

JUNIPER: What were the other questions like? Were they nicer than that one?

SAGE: I don't think that's true. This album is nerdy as shit.

HOLLY: For the record, I voted against the Cake Wizard song

SAGE: You literally wrote that song. And the Vexington one. Most of the nerdy shit in this album is stuff you wrote.

HOLLY: So, what you're saying, Sage, is that *you're* the Fake Geek Girl.

JUNIPER: When we started, being a geeky band was what set us apart. But the geek identity has changed a lot over the last few years. Being nerdy has more mainstream appeal than it used to.
SAGE: Universal themes, baby!

*Breakfast TV is hilarious. They clearly have no idea who the
band is or why they might be popular. Then one host got the idea
of bringing in her teen daughter to do the interview.*

TARA: OMG, that Witchstarter campaign was incredible, I
couldn't take my eyes off it.
HOLLY: Our fans are so awesome. What we didn't expect was
how many new fans we would find because of the campaign.
TARA: Did you ever doubt you'd reach your goal?
SAGE: We had smart people helping us, running the numbers.
We figured we'd get there. But we didn't know how big it was
going to get.
JUNIPER: I still don't believe it.

————

SAGE

Sure, I've got better things to do on a Saturday morning than
stare at a mirror that's lying flat on the kitchen table. Maybe
Holly does too.

If we were smart about it, we'd take shifts. So we could take turns at a normal life. But since when have we made smart choices?

"Are you two still staring at that thing?" asks Dec on his way out the door.

He's wearing his date shirt. A lesser human being might take time away from this important mirror-staring to tease him about that. But no, not today. Today, I live for the mirror.

There's a big number on the screen. Every now and then, it gets higher. Sometimes Hol lets out a shrill squeaking sound. Sometimes my foot twitches.

The number is everything.

Somewhere, a door bangs open.

"Honestly, you two," says Hebes, putting something that smells amazing down on the counter. "Did you even think about food? Or water? Or taking breaks? A watched cauldron doesn't boil."

"That's where you're wrong, Hebes," I inform her. "Turns out? This watched cauldron is boiling. And bubbling. Turning everyone to newts. If we look away it might stop. We're here for the duration. Deal with it."

"You really shouldn't…" She pauses. Caught by the mesmeric stare of the number. "Holy crap."

"Yep."

"That's… you've already blown past your goal. It's the first day, Sage. How is that even… oh it went up!"

"You see!" Holly says, smacking the table. "It keeps doing that."

"It's so much money," Hebe breathes.

She sits down at the table, completely forgetting about the food she brought us.

And then it's three of us, staring at a mirror.

———

Mei: Witchstarter

Sage: Bless you

Mei: Seriously, Sage. You've done some crowdfunding before. But Witchstarter is a game changer. You could fund the new album, easy. Didn't Holly want to tour this year?

Sage: Eh, i don't know. We did okay raising money last time but it's a lot of work

Mei: Do it. I'll handle the spreadsheets for you. DO IT.

Sage: fine, whatever. How's Paris?

Mei: dreamy

Sage: tell Viola to post back my fucking t-shirt she stole again

Mei: don't pretend you didn't already convey that message through song

———

FROM THE DIARY OF MISS JUNIPER CRESSWELL, WITCH

Some time past noon, I awoke to find myself tucked into bed. Perplexed, I wandered up to the kitchen of residence above. "Holly, did you drug me?"

"I put a tiny sleeping hex on your hot chocolate," replied my delightful girlfriend, sitting in a tight huddle with Sage and Hebe.

"*Holly.*"

"You were stressed, love. I don't like to see you all worked up like that."

"Of course I'm stressed," I said crossly. "The Witchstarter goes live today. What if everyone hates it? What if they laugh at us? What if it's a huge mistake... why are you all staring at that mirror?"

No one said anything. It occurred to me belatedly that it was now today.

"Ah," I said, peering at the number on the screen. That was a terribly large number. "My goodness."

"Sit down, babe," says Holly. "We're going to be staring at this mirror for the next 29 days, okay?"

"Sounds fair," I said, and managed to put the kettle on before I was also drawn into the mesmeric stare of Fake Geek Girl's epic Witchstarter campaign.

CHAPTER FOUR

FAKE GEEK GIRL VS SONGS ABOUT YOUR RELATIONSHIP STATUS

MORTICIA GLOOM: This is 7X666, Harpy Radio, and I have the lead singer of Fake Geek Girl here in the studio, Holly Hallow!

HOLLY: Hi, Morticia. Love your show!

MORTICIA: I bet you do, we've been playing your songs all week

HOLLY: Oh? Haaaadn't noticed.

MORTICIA: This album is just packed with feelings. Are any of the songs based on real people?

HOLLY: It is legit that everyone's kissed our drummer.

MORTICIA: We've got to talk about the coffee song.

HOLLY: Yeah, nah, that's a play by play of how Sage and his boyfriend got together. The song is slightly less dramatic.

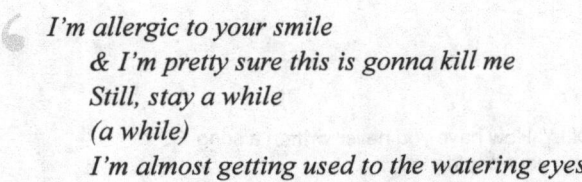

> *I'm allergic to your smile*
> > *& I'm pretty sure this is gonna kill me*
> > *Still, stay a while*
> > *(a while)*
> > *I'm almost getting used to the watering eyes*

————

SAGE

Jules Nightshade fighting frost trolls in the street was one of the hottest things I'd ever seen in my life. He was like a beautiful streak of lightning in the middle of a rainstorm, all power and sarcasm and ice-cold magic.

I wanted to rip his clothes off. Mess his hair up. I settled for backing him into the wall, and kissing him when he threw his arms around my neck.

That's where it started, I guess.

JULES

Sage must never know that I had a crush on him for months before we met at Medea's Cauldron. I used to make Vale take me to watch that bloody band.

Life was a hell of a lot easier when he was the hot drummer I was never, ever going to speak to.

VIOLA

Literally neither of them remembers that I was also there that night. By the way, when they were so busy eating each other's faces off against the brick wall, guess who finished off the trolls for them?

You're welcome, Fake Geek Girl fans. I'm the only reason your drummer didn't get pounded by a frost troll.

Ahem. So to speak.

————

HOLLY: How have you never written a song about your boyfriend?

SAGE: I don't write love songs. No one needs that paper trail

HOLLY: Mate, I'm making you look bad

SAGE: You know we can't put fourteen "I'm in love with Juniper" songs on the same album, right? They won't all fit. I'm pretty sure most of them are the same song.

SAGE: Apart from anything else, Juniper has also written a song, and it's kind of great, gotta budge up to make room for it

HOLLY: OMG have you read it? Is it about me?

SAGE: Mostly it's about dresses with pockets in I think? Didn't really pay attention to the lyrics. We've been working on the melody and structure though, it's gonna be great. might even talk her into singing it.

HOLLY: My girlfriend wrote a song about… pockets?

SAGE: It's possible you are the pockets. I don't know. I don't get metaphor. But it's got a kicky beat.

———

I saw a girl out walking with a
    Beautiful smile
    and she said: "I like your dress"
I replied: "Thanks, it has pockets

———

SAGE: hey hol

HOLLY: r you seriously texting me right now we are in the same room

SAGE: do you think its weird I haven't written a
song about jules

HOLLY: album's not done yet

HOLLY: still time

SAGE: what would I even say?

HOLLY: i don't know talk about his hair

SAGE: enough with the hair songs, Holly, it's
creepy

SAGE: he'd probably hate it anyway

HOLLY: tell you what, if we get 1000 backers on
Witchstarter, you write a song about jules
fricking nightshade and I get to put one of my
Juniper is the best thing since sliced bread
songs on the album

SAGE: can it be one of the geeky ones

HOLLY: they're all geeky, you people have
ruined me for life

SAGE: no way we get 1000 backers

SAGE: that's crazysauce

HOLLY: so?

SAGE: you're on

———

Don't say you love me
  Your magic is crawling under my skin (my skin)
  & I don't think you understand
  What a bloody awful nightmare situation we
are in

———

Toil & Trouble LIVE: Coffee is the Key to Surviving You is being talked about everywhere. Ella from Metal Headed Wombats described it as the best anti-love song she'd ever heard. What was your inspiration?

SAGE: I just find it really annoying to be in a solid healthy relationship with the hottest person I've ever met. Never tell him I said that.

Toil & Trouble LIVE: This is a live interview.

SAGE: It's fine, he's probably not watching.

———

"Trainee Agent Nightshade, turn off that fucking livestream and pay attention to the actual surveillance cameras."

"Sorry, Agent Jones. My boyfriend is being sweet on the internet."

"Your boyfriend is a menace to society, that's what he is."

"Also true."

———

> *Your mouth on mine was a terrible idea*
> *Your hand in mine is a hell of a sight*
> *Pour a cup of coffee, love*
> *& maybe the two of us will live through this*
> *night*

CHAPTER FIVE
FAKE GEEK GIRL VS GUEST INSTRUMENTALS

HECATE MAC: So, Juniper. You're a classically trained musician. What are you doing in a rock band?

JUNIPER: I fell in with a bad crowd. Best thing that ever happened to me.

HOLLY: Awww.

HECATE MAC: You have some guest artists on this album for the first time! Tell us about your collab with the Belladonna U Lake Monster.

JUNIPER: That was Holly's idea.

HOLLY: I met Sofia when I was working on Star Magic, and I knew she was going to be huge.

HECATE MAC: You knew her before she was famous?

HOLLY: She knew me before I was famous! I was writing Love Song for Cryptids, Sofia sort of stole my boyfriend at the time, I figured out I was in love with Juniper, it was a whole thing. Sofia has always been connected to this song, whether she knew it or not. We were stoked she came on to do guest vocals for the track.

HECATE MAC: I have, so many followup questions.

JUNIPER: Nora! She was part of the band from the beginning, but left a while ago for her own projects. We invited her back to bring some keyboards back into the Fake Geek Girl sound.

HOLLY: Plus it was her idea to do a disco remix of Stupid Songs About Victorian Novels as one of our Witchstarter exclusive reward tracks! Love you, Nora.

HECATE MAC: Who plays the piano on "Vex Me?" It's unusual for you to leave an artist uncredited, and it's such an integral part of the song.

HOLLY: Piano? What piano? No idea what you're talking about.

JUNIPER: I'm afraid we're taking that secret to the grave.

SAGE: Send help my boyfriend did something so hot I can't stand it but also I want to kill him

HOLLY: (attaches lyrics in progress for Cauldron Full of Cats)

SAGE: No shut up you are the only person I can tell

SAGE: I went to his mum's fancy hotel for dinner & irene has this stupid rich person apartment that's like five hotel suites glued together

HOLLY: go on

HOLLY: also Jules' mum is hot

SAGE: she owns a grand piano

HOLLY: please tell Jules it is a good thing I got a steady gf before I was informed of this fact which only makes his mum hotter

SAGE: nononono she doesn't play it

SAGE: it's basically random furniture for her and sometimes she hires concert pianists for parties

HOLLY: awesome, continue

SAGE: but then

SAGE: she told me

SAGE: "of course Jules used to make use of it, but he never plays for me anymore"

SAGE: [head exploding dancemoji]

HOLLY: YOUR STUPID BOYFRIEND CAN PLAY THE MOFO PIANO

HOLLY: !!!!!!!

SAGE sorry got a bit distracted

HOLLY its been 2 hours where were you

SAGE I just found out my bf took like 10 years of piano lessons there were CONSEQUENCES

SAGE sex consequences

HOLLY ew overshare

HOLLY he knows we're gonna gang up on him & force him play a track on the next album right

SAGE he's aware

SAGE: !!!!!!! ferd you arsehole how could you not tell me jules can play piano this is a major betrayal from you, friendship cancelled

FERD: u know vale did like 12 years of harp right? there were competitions n everything

SAGE: ...

_____

> SAGE: [customised harp dancemoji]

> VIOLA VALE: no

> SAGE: [dancing harp, dancing harp, giant kitten eyes, magic wand)

> VIOLA VALE: fuck off sage

_____

HECATE MAC: I believe you also have an uncredited harpist on your Regency Ballroom dance mix version of Witches Roll Dice, Bitches, another Witchstarter exclusive track. Any comment?

HOLLY: Funny story, turns out Sage plays the harp.

JUNIPER: Sweetheart, stop lying about Sage on the radio, it makes him tetchy.

HOLLY: Funny story, turns out I play the harp.

_____

DRAGONATOR: Third most popular question from our poll: what do you guys have against guitars anyway?

HOLLY: Guitars are for cowards.

CHAPTER SIX
FAKE GEEK GIRL VS THE BASILISK SONG

BREAKFAST TV TARA: The Basilisk Song is so sad!

SAGE: That one's not about my boyfriend!

HOLLY: Sure it's not.

JUNIPER: It's our most collaborative song. A lot of shared experience in there, of us, of our friends. That's why the co-writing credits.

SAGE: The people you date at uni, or high school or whatever, aren't always the people you spend your life with. Unless you're lucky, and they stick around as friends. Or… whatever.

HOLLY: Yeah, whatever. It's a big-arse growing up song with loads of cello instrumentals.

BREAKFAST TV TARA: Doesn't that describe all of your songs?

———

    hello, how are you, I'm fine
       I guess you are wondering what's on my mind
       you look so familiar there across the room
       and your name is on the tip of my tongue
       you turn your head a touch too soon

and I swear the air punches right out of my
lungs

———

"So," said Hebe. "Europe."

Ferd sat opposite her at the Fennysnake Cafe. He had ordered pancakes and mushrooms but didn't eat either. She had ordered cheesy rosemary waffles and eaten half of them already.

"I know it isn't great timing," he said. "For us."

"Mm." Understatement of the year.

They'd been moving towards something, she thought. Something new and... not *better* than before. But something with a little more solidity to it. She'd seen the shape of a future together.

Apparently, he was looking in another direction.

"You know what it's been like," he said. "Every job interview since I graduated has brought up my parents, the scandal, the court case... they should be in prison, but someone pulled strings somewhere to make their criminal charges disappear. I keep getting all these — fucking encouraging messages from their old friends, who are all totally spying on me. Everyone thinks I'm still on their side, that I'm part of that world."

"I know all this," Hebe said, rolling her eyes. "I don't need the power point presentation, Ferd. I get it. It's Europe. Why wouldn't you go?"

She wasn't going to ask if he was planning on coming back.

"I just really need to get out of this bloody country for a while," he said, sounding so apologetic it made her want to stab him with a fork."

"I'm not holding you back," she said impatiently. "What do you want me to do, beg you to stay?"

"That's not fair."

She cut her remaining waffles into tiny squares and then triangles, wondering why she was even annoyed by this.

"You could come with me," Ferd suggested in a low voice. "Have an adventure together."

Hebe sighed. "I don't think that's a good idea."

———

we went through hell
I remember it well
and by the end I wasn't even sure that you
liked me
but we stayed friends
that's the worst thing about it
friends aren't supposed to stop texting hello

———

FERD: Thanks for the lift, mate.

SAGE: np, you get through security OK?

FERD: it's a miracle

SAGE: cool cool let me know if you need a rescue crew

SAGE: tell Vale to post me back my fucken t-shirt, I know she stole it again before she left

FERD: yeah you're never seeing that again

SAGE: don't tell Hebe I told you but she looks sad

FERD: cheers

SAGE: I mention it cos for a bloke about to jet off to the other side of the country you look pretty fucken sad too

FERD: [doc attached]

SAGE: fckit you are sitting in an airport writing tragic song lyrics about the one that got away. het romance is the worst

SAGE: not too late to run through that airport backwards and go get your girl

FERD: already on the plane

SAGE: you dickhead

SAGE: good lyrics though I'm stealing them for the new album

FERD: [thumbs up]

———

let's catch up, pour a wine
how are your friends, how are mine?
no one's fault, such a shame
we lost touch, I guess it happens
and I really wish I could remember your name

CHAPTER SEVEN
FAKE GEEK GIRL VS MEDUSA

PIERS VALENTINE: The album cover for Like Witches For Coffee is outstanding. Who came up with the idea for the snake-haired wigs?
HOLLY: Viola Vale, with two Vs…
JUNIPER: We have some really creative friends. Declan from Maenad Design let us use some of his sculptures for the photo shoot, and we all love getting dressed up.
SAGE: I look good in snakes.
JUNIPER: Annie Tuesday is our very talented photographer, she made us all look so great. The coffee mugs were provided by Aurora from Teal, a fabulous boutique in the city…

———

VALE: tell Holly to stop talking about me in interviews, no one needs to know about my embarrassing brief interlude in your stupid dice-rolling cult

SAGE: she says stop stalking us online and maybe she will

SAGE: where's my t-shirt, witch?

VALE: write a song about it, loser

VALE: oh, wait, you did

VALE: so this Annie, she's Dec's new gf, yeah?

SAGE: super casual the way you dropped that into conversation

SAGE: proud of you babe

VALE: fuck you Sage

VALE: gonna take a bath in your t-shirt while drinking red wine

SAGE: i knew you had it, you vixen!!!!!!!

SAGE: see you on Sat for virtual D&D?

VALE: no

VALE: maybe

> I said, don't go
>> Be my friend, stay at home
>> don't steal my fucking t-shirts just to keep a
> piece of me
>> your place is here
>> just here
>> there's a room waiting for you
>> if you had to leave, couldn't you take me too?

CHAPTER EIGHT

FAKE GEEK GIRL VS EVERYONE'S KISSED THE DRUMMER

CERYS UP LATE: So, I have to ask about the song Everyone's Kissed the Drummer...

SAGE: Holly Hallow is a liar.

HOLLY: What do you think? Would you trust this face?

SAGE: I'm a trustworthy person. And an excellent kisser.

JUNIPER: We felt it's important to have a song on the album that's kind of stupid so people can embarrass Sage by requesting it at live shows.

HOLLY: And on the bus as it turns out. In the street. At the supermarket.

JUNIPER: In related news, we will never again offer a bonus reward of "name a track on the album" in future Witchstarter campaigns. That's on us.

HOLLY: I mean, that's what got Dec to pledge to the campaign. Totes worth it.

SAGE: Dec named that song? Dec paid five hundred bucks to name that song? [expletive deleted for broadcast]

HOLLY: This is why artists aren't supposed to earn a living wage. Money gives them too much power.

VIOLA: saw the latest FGG interview! what I'm taking from this is that you also have kissed Sage

DEC: Spin the bottle, two years ago.

VIOLA: Too much tongue, right?

DEC: Way too much tongue. How's Paris?

VIOLA: Fabulous. How's life as a moderately successful sculptor?

DEC: I think I have arthritis in my elbows

VIOLA: See, watercolourists don't have that problem. How's Annie?

DEC: She's good. Still won't let me draw her. Says she doesn't want to end up in my gallery of granite ex-girlfriends

VIOLA: You should marry her

DEC: Smart, I hadn't thought of that. How's Claude?

VIOLA: All good. Look at us, we're so fucking mature

DEC: [high-five]

VIOLA: nope, I take it back, you're twelve

Draft lyrics:

> *Everyone's kissed the drummer*
> *In that band you like*
> *He's not that special*
> *Don't get attached*
> *See that girl?*

She kissed the drummer
It was a terrible life choice and now she's in
a *song*
See that boy?
He kissed the drummer
(So did his brother)

Too soon?

CHAPTER NINE
FAKE GEEK GIRL VS
CAULDRON FULL OF CATS

CERYS UP LATE: So many love songs on this album.

HOLLY: We love love.

CERYS UP LATE: And you're all in happy relationships — Holly and Juniper are together, Sage has his mysterious nameless boyfriend…

HOLLY: Does he even exist? Who knows. Maybe he is also a cryptid.

JUNIPER: This is absolutely an album of love songs. Not just romantic love. A lot of our music is about the love you have for your friends. The people who hold you up. The people who stay in your life as you figure out what kind of adult you want to be.

HOLLY: Also the back-stabbing so-called mates who make fun of you for being in a happy relationship because that makes for boring songs, *apparently*

CERYS UP LATE: I was gonna say, there's something… almost domestic about some of these songs?

HOLLY: I think it's stupid to assume you can't make good art out of being happy. Sourdough bread, holding hands with your honey, communicating about your problems. That shit is punk.

CERYS UP LATE: Juniper, would you agree with that?

[Juniper is staring at Holly]

JUNIPER: Sorry, I was just… distracted by how smart my girl-friend is. What was the question?

———

> *No one wants to hear about happy ever after*
>   *You rescued the damsel*
>   *The princess is in your castle*
>   *Congratulations*
>   *(congratu-fucking-lations)*
>   *You got to the end*

———

SAGE: These are all the same fucking song, Holly

HOLLY: You are not limiting me to one Juniper love song when your stupid squishy Jules feels are jizzed all over this album

JUNIPER: can I not be in this group chat, please?

———

> *Your friends are all bored with your cottagecore romance*
>   *A cauldron full of cats and*
>   *Roses grown wild round the door*
>   *You overcame your shortcomings*
>   *And she overlooked all your flaws*

———

JUNIPER: I think Sage is right

HOLLY: Et too, brutal?

JUNIPER: would it have killed you to take one English Lit class? Never mind

JUNIPER: The cauldron full of cats song and the gaming song about the princess reward, they're the same song! At least, they could be

JUNIPER: I think if you combine them, they're better

JUNIPER [document attached]

HOLLY: holy Miss Hardbroom, I'm in love with a songwriting genius

———

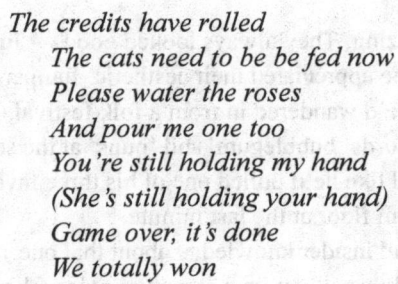

The credits have rolled
     The cats need to be be fed now
     Please water the roses
And pour me one too
You're still holding my hand
(She's still holding your hand)
Game over, it's done
We totally won

CHAPTER TEN

FAKE GEEK GIRL LIVE IN CONCERT (WITCHSTARTER EXCLUSIVE)

The band looked amazing. They always looked good — Jules might be biased, but he appreciated their aesthetic. Juniper as always looked like she'd wandered in from a folk festival, Holly made you think the words 'bubblegum' and 'punk' at the same time, and Sage looked like he'd pulled one of his three favourite t-shirts off the bedroom floor at the last minute.

(Possibly, Jules had insider knowledge about that one.)

They made it work: usually with a signature colour they shared. Tonight it was yellow, Sage's vintage t-shirt from a band everyone forgot in the 90s balancing out Holly's bright lemon tank top over a tiny plaid skirt and fishnets, and Juniper's long hand-made skirt covered in sunflowers.

The Hellbroth was full of diehard Fake Geek Girl fans who had funded the album by snapping up tickets to this Witchstarter backer-exclusive show.

It was hot and sweaty and Jules had assumed his mother would hate it.

(He had rather banked on her saying a polite no when he asked her, but she patted his hand and told him that *actually* she had bought her own ticket, how did he think the Fake Geek Girl Kickstarter hit their first thousand dollars so quickly.)

Sage leaned into his microphone, taking back the lead singer role from Holly while still seated at his drums. "Hey all, this is one of the songs you really liked on this album…" he started to say.

The crowd roared.

Jules wondered if Mother would notice if he sidled away outside for this part; he didn't particularly want anyone he knew watching his reaction if Sage got romantic.

On the other hand, Mother was wearing blue jeans for what he was pretty certain was the first time this century, paired with a David Bowie t-shirt that looked alarmingly worn in, and if Jules left her side he was going to have to live with the consequences of her being hit on by several of his friends.

"Yeah, yeah," Sage laughed, quietening the crowd. "It's the fucking coffee song. I'm getting to it. Holly sings it on the album and she does a bang up, kickass take on it."

"You noticed?" said their actual lead singer, smirking at him.

Sage waved her away from him. "Get off, witch, no one's stealing your solos." He looked back to the crowd, turning up that charisma of his. Jules had no idea how he did it, but the power of Sage performing always hit him in the back teeth. The only thing close to it he'd experienced in life was watching Sage perform magic: every bit as hot, and overwhelming.

"It's no secret that we wrote this one for me," Sage went on. "One of the most popular requests for this exclusive backer-only gig was to hear me sing it in person."

There was shrieking in the crowd now. Legit screaming. Jules was glad Vale and Chauv were too far away to witness this. If only he could teleport Mother away to join them in Paris…

"Nah, I'm not telling you who I'm singing it to," Sage teased his fans. He blew a random kiss into the crowd, aiming it nowhere near Jules. Nice touch. "Oh, there he was, too bad, gone now. I guess I don't have to sing it after all…"

The crowd definitely had opinions about that.

"Right," said Sage, grinning wildly. There was a line of

sweat across his forehead. Tragically it did not make him less attractive. "Fuck it, let's go. This one's for J, he knows who he is. Can we can make him blush all over?"

The drums started, Juniper's cello strings rose to meet the song, and Sage started singing.

Later, much later, as the band and their closest people wound down over coffee and chocolate, sprawling over several booths in the now-closed-to-customers pub side of the Hellbroth venue, Jules asked Mother what she thought of the show.

Irene Nightshade, who generally spent her Saturday nights at art openings, charity fundraisers and the opera, gave him a slightly patronising smile. "I don't mean to criticise your life-style, darling," she said, always a good start. "But did you consider that maybe, given your position in covert government intelligence, it not the *best* idea to date a rock star?"

"I'm not dating a rock star," Jules said grumpily into his mug of mocha, which helped to dampen the magical sparks flicking in his general direction from his boyfriend, several seats away. "I'm dating *Sage*."

"And the difference is…"

Jules as confused. Mother adored Sage. He'd almost been expecting her to start on wedding hints rather than whatever this was.

"Is there something else you wanted to say?" he suggested.

An odd look crossed her face. "It's nothing you need to worry about, dear."

"Ironically, the most worrying statement I've heard all night."

Mother sipped on her cocktail. Everyone else was on beer, coffee or chocolate, because it was two in the morning, but Mother had somehow convinced the bartender (who usually offered cocktails named after fictional spaceships) to produce her favourite cocktail: a Manhattan with a frozen sphere of pomegranate seeds suspended on a cocktail stick instead of a cherry.

"I may be having some trouble with the Board," she admitted. "Not your concern."

"It kind of is, though," said Jules, narrowing his eyes at her. "Is this the retirement bullshit again?"

His control freak of a grandfather had recently declared his upcoming retirement, throwing the Nightshade/Morgana Group Hotel Empire into what could only be described as a flap.

"My lawyers are handling it," Mother said prissily.

"Always a sign of things going well."

Irene Nightshade had always been intended to succeed Julius, carrying on his legacy. But it had been clear for a long time that the elderly warlocks on the Board had only ever intended her to be a placeholder for the 'true' heir — and Jules had been turning down their overtures since he was eighteen.

Ugh, this was what came from belonging to an 'old' family. From the outside it looked all marvellous with the money and the shiny broomsticks and the hotel empire but as as soon as you scratched the surface you found it was based on ancient contracts, blood debt, and *oh, we promised our firstborn son to a djinn.*

"It's not just that you won't accept your seat on the Board..."

"Good, because my job literally will not allow me to do that."

"But rumours spread, dear. I adore Sage. But he's not exactly... future husband of the Chair of the Board material."

"Good," said Jules savagely. "Since you're going to be the Chair for the next fifty fucking years as far as I'm concerned."

"I know that, and you know that," said Irene Nightshade. "But tell those nasty old goblins the truth and they'll all start sharpening their knives for my back."

"Promise them my firstborn," Jules suggested. "Pledge the next generation of Nightshades to the Board."

"Darling," Mother said, looking startled. "That's a lot to put on a child who isn't even born yet."

"You think?"

"I take it this is your way of telling me you don't plan to give me grandchildren. You know the gay thing doesn't need to stand in your way."

"Well aware, Mother. But between his job and my job, it's not a conversation we're likely to have for a decade or more."

"Fine," she sighed, letting the last drop of cocktail fall into her mouth. "But if you trip and fall on adoption papers, your *children* will have a hotel empire to run."

"Don't threaten me with a good time."

"Hey," said Sage, swooping in from the other booth to crowd up against Jules' side, still holding his beer. "What are we talking about?"

Mother smiled brilliantly, looking completely sincere. "Sage, darling. Loved your show. Will you sign my CD?"

————

Viola felt her mirror hum as she headed down into the underground tunnel of the Metro. She pulled it out to answer, since she had a few minutes to kill before her train. "Nightshade. Congrats on getting the time zones right for once."

Jules looked like he was coming down off a long night, his hair rumpled and his eyeliner smudged. "Vale."

"What's wrong?"

"I'm dating a fucking rock star. Is that… going to be a problem, do you think?"

She smirked at him. "Don't you think that's a little over-dramatic? They're barely even famous."

Across the tracks, a train moved on its way to reveal a massive wall-covering billboard beyond. The faces of Sage,

Holly and Juniper stared back at her, framed by the snakes of three Medusa wigs.

The new album, loud and proud. All the way on the other side of the world.

"Oh, fuck," Viola breathed. "Jules. You might be dating a rock star."

CHAPTER ELEVEN
FAKE GEEK GIRL VS ONE TRUE PAIRINGS

GINGER TATE: It's six months since Like Witches For Coffee was released worldwide, smashing chart expectations. What's next for Fake Geek Girl?
SAGE: We're still doing this!
HOLLY: Touring, baby, all the way.
JUNIPER: I'm thinking about taking up a postgraduate degree part-time… but you probably weren't asking about that.

———

Paris Viola looked amazing. Her hair was ridiculously stylish, and while she was almost certainly wearing clothes she had brought with her from Australia, somehow they looked even more put together.

Hebe, just off the worst long haul flight she'd ever experienced, felt like yesterday's pyjamas dressed up in last year's jeans.

"Coming through!" said Mei, seizing Hebe's suitcase and hauling it into the world's tiniest apartment.

"There's almost no space," Viola said, sounding almost

apologetic. "Chauvelin pretty much had to fold himself in half to sleep on our couch."

"Ferd's not here now?" Hebe asked, to be polite. Not internally screaming at all.

"Don't tell me you're here for him!" said Mei from a kitchen so small you could barely stand a baguette up in it. "Wait until you see these croissants, they're so big you have to assume they ate a bunch of other croissants on their way here."

"I'm here to see you," Hebe sputtered. "Obviously. And France. I've never been to France before. I wouldn't come all this way for… you know. Some stupid romantic gesture or anything."

Both women looked at her as if they could see all the way through last year's jeans to her soul.

"This is going to require wine," said Viola finally. "So much wine."

————

SAGE: no

SAGE: not allowed

SAGE: I can't write another fucking song about a mate who leaves the country I'll start looking tragic

HEBE: cool your hexes, Sage

HEBE: I bought a return ticket. I'll be home in six weeks

HEBE: I'm not even gonna miss D&D night because the mirrorweb exists

SAGE: oh

SAGE: guess I'm the arsehole then

HEBE: and there's your next album title

———

"Europe Chauvelin is much easier to deal with than Australia Chauvelin," said Viola, two hours later. She had changed from the little black dress that was apparently her 'work costume' into Sage's old Kraken t-shirt and pyjama pants. She still looked like she belonged on the front of a magazine. "Apparently what it took for him to chill the fuck out was being as far away from his parents as humanly possible."

"Cheers to that," said Mei, who had taken to clinking her wine glass at any excuse.

"Can't say it's done me any harm either," Viola added. "If only I could get Jules on a plane he might finally stop worrying about his mother's hotel inheritance issues and get on with being happy."

"Rich witch problems," Mei agreed solemnly.

"He's in Florence right now," Viola added. "He left for Italy a month ago. But I swear he checks in with me more per week than he did for like, the last two years put together."

"I haven't heard from him," Hebe confessed. "I thought maybe… but it's stupid."

Viola gave her a look over her wineglass,. For a moment, she looked like every Macbeth's witch who ever leaned ominously over a cauldron. "He asked you to come with him, didn't he?"

Hebe shrugged. "I'm happy where I am, and he's so busy running away from everything it's hard to pin him down for a conversation. We're not in the same place right now — lifewise, not just, you know. Florence."

"Mmhmm," said Viola, playing with her phone. "Not that what you're saying isn't fascinating, but oh look, I just booked you a train trip to a random city in Italy, how's that for a fun holiday idea?"

"I hate you," said Hebe.

"You say that now," said Viola. "But I don't think you understand quite how much excellent wine we have packed into this shoebox of a flat."

———

SAGE: how's italy?

HEBE: the coffee is to die for I think my magic is gone forever

SAGE: and Ferd?

HEBE: he seems happy

SAGE: fucker

HEBE: I know, right? how dare he

SAGE: not allowed

HEBE: how are you doing?

SAGE: I never want to talk about one of my songs ever ever again in the whole of ever

HEBE: oh poor baby

HEBE: is success a terrible burden?

SAGE: oi I don't need you to poke holes in my ego

SAGE: I have people to do that for me now

SAGE: semi famous indie rock star I'll have you know

HEBE: star is a stretch

SAGE: I said SEMI famous

SAGE: come home

HEBE: six weeks, you'll live

SAGE: love you

HEBE: ti amo

SAGE: bring back some of that fancy Italian coffee

HEBE: add it to your rider, rock star

———

Hebe awoke in a beautiful hotel room with a view over an exquisite Florentine garden. She couldn't quite see the Arno from the balcony window… but it would do.

"Where are you?" she asked sleepily.

The windows opened and Ferd walked in from the balcony, bringing in their dessert glasses from the night before. He wore satiny pyjama shorts and nothing else, so mostly what she saw was an expanse of warm brown skin, his dark hair, and his new tattoo — a line of Latin poetry that curved over the top of his right hip.

She felt like a character in a novel.

"Just checking to see if all the extra throw pillows migrated in the night," he said with a relaxed grin. "The hotel should give us a discount on this, really."

"Shut up," Hebe said, throwing one of the pillows at his face, since that was what they were designed for. "I can't help it if my magic creates soft furnishings when I'm happy."

His face did something really good at that — as if he had been holding a final knot of tension in his shoulders which now completely disappeared. "Happy, eh?"

"Don't let it go to your head. Gelato and a good night's sleep has that effect on me."

"Room service breakfast?"

"Oh, if we have to, I suppose. Those things that aren't croissants."

"Cornetti."

"I want those. And if you pour more coffee into me, the throw pillow issue will take care of itself."

"Then how will I know you're happy?"

"If I'm eating cornetti, you can just take my happiness as read."

———

After a lazy breakfast on the balcony, in which Ferd's bare foot kept brushing against Hebe's bare calf, she finally asked him what she had been thinking since she first discovered where he was staying.

"How on earth can you afford this? I thought you were back-packing!"

"Two answers to that. The first one is — Irene Nightshade owns this hotel. She offered to comp me while I'm away, so my tour of Europe is very much based around which cities have hotels that come under the Morgana Group banner."

"*Oh*. Well, she's welcome to keep the extra throw pillows. I like Irene."

Ferd tilted his head back, dark eyes looking wary. "Second answer is — I got a job."

"Oh." More muted this time. Hebe felt something tight and hard build in her chest. *That was fast.* When Ferd left, she had known it was likely he would find somewhere to settle down, somewhere that wasn't home, but it had only been a few months. "What kind of job?" she managed to ask.

Ferd looked troubled. "The kind I promised myself I wouldn't take when I graduated. Working for one of my fucking uncles. He swears he won't use it to manipulate me or force me to be in a room with my parents, but..." He shrugged.

"Didn't you leave Australia to avoid family connections?" she couldn't help asking.

Ferd winced. "Yeah, miscalculated there. Half my family is French."

"The job's in France? What will you be doing?" Hebe had been working retail jobs for years. She could pretend to be enthusiastic about *anything*.

"You're looking at the Unreal Consultant to Pierre Diallo Financials International. I get to sit in board rooms and tell them how their policies affect employees and customers who don't have magic."

"I mean," said Hebe. "It sounds… useful? And relevant to your degree."

"I fully expect to be miserable and frustrated within six months," Ferd said, attempting to steal the last of the cornetti from the shared platter, and giving her heart-eyes when Hebe threatened him with the fork. He broke it in half, giving her the larger piece.

So now she had heart-eyes.

"Why do it if you think you'll end up hating it?" she asked.

"The salary is fuck off levels of incredible," Ferd muttered. "If I'm lucky I'll get head-hunted within a year or two and get to work for a company where my boss isn't related to me. And, uh. It's in Melbourne. Probably should have mentioned that."

Hebe stopped chewing. "What?" she said, letting crumbs fly everywhere. "*What?*"

He was practically vibrating with internal conflict. "I miss everyone, and travelling around Europe on your own is really fucking miserable when you think you can't go home, and everyone takes shitty jobs when they're young, what kind of arsehole am I to complain about doing this for a couple of years while I keep an eye out for something better… oh, lap!"

Yes, indeed, Hebe was in his lap. Well spotted, Unreal Consultant.

"You're coming home," she breathed.

"I have eight more weeks before I have to start," Ferd said, kissing her neck, apparently not caring at all about the cornetti crumbs situation. "What about you?"

"My flight home is in twenty days. I wasn't planning to go beyond France..."

"Irene Nightshade owns hotels in Crete, Barcelona, Vienna, Prague and Marseilles. Plus I reckon we can crash on Vale's floor again if you need more time in Paris."

"Huh," said Hebe. "My boss did say I could... take more time if I wanted."

"Can you change your flight?"

"Mmm," said Hebe. "I mean, not right now. I'm busy kissing you. But I'll think about it."

FERD'S NEW TATTOO:
Non est ad astra mollis e terris via
   (*there is no easy way from the earth to the*
   *star*s)

SENECA

"I feel guilty running out on you for a boy," Hebe protested, the night before she took the train from Paris to Florence to see Ferd.

"Ugh, like you two aren't one of my OTPs," Mei said, laughing at her.

"Is that a nerd thing?" asked Viola, like they hadn't just spent an hour talking about the function of the Coffeelock in D&D.

"One True Pairing," explained Mei.

"Ugh, there's no such thing. Soulmates bullshit. Relationships take work." Viola waved her wineglass. "Everyone thought Chauv and I going to be the perfect couple, our parents were obsessed with us getting together. Such a fucking lucky escape for me, no offence."

"None taken," said Hebe, swallowing a laugh.

"Parents shipping their kids together is creepy," Mei agreed.

"Having said that," Viola went on. "As it turns out, my soul-mate right now is three different hot Frenchmen, all called Claude. The world is a magnificent place."

"Mine is a new forum I found that's entirely dedicated to Cake Wizards coffee shop AUs!" said Mei. "Our love will be eternal."

"I don't think I agree with OTPs," Hebe said thoughtfully. "In fic or in real life. I was always more interested in stories about the rare pairs."

"So like, Sage and Viola," Mei suggested.

"Ew," said Viola. "Bitch, please."

"I don't care if Ferd is my soulmate or not," Hebe went on. "I just — I miss him. I don't think we're done yet. So I suppose I'd better find out."

"In Florrrrrrence?" Viola teased.

"Since you already bought me the ticket, yes, fine. Why not Florence? I promised myself I'd add things to the bucket list of brave on this trip.Hopping on a train to Florence for a date with my ex has to count."

"Eh," said Viola. "If Chauvelin turns out to be a bust, I recommend picking a hot Italian to have a fling with. The scenery will be nice, either way."

SAGE: hey hebes

SAGE: Hebe Edna Hallow, pay attention to me!

SAGE: HEBE WILHELMINA GERTRUDE VON HALLOWSTEIN!!!!

HEBE: ???

HEBE: wtf sage

SAGE: oh hellow hebes I have a brilliant idea

HEBE: it's 4 in the morning here in italy

HEBE: you dick

SAGE: you're the one reading your texts at 4 in the morning, this is on you

SAGE: so

SAGE: and bear with me on this

SAGE: have you ever thought about learning to play guitar?

———

HEBE: you need to fire your drummer

HOLLY: ok good call

HOLLY: does this mean he asked you about the guitar thing?

HOLLY: because he may be on to something, we can always do with a second set of strings

HOLLY: or keyboards mbbe?

HOLLY: Hebe?

HOLLY: Heeeeeeeeebe?

HOLLY: yeah k I'll let you sleep

HOLLY: [customised witch playing guitar dancemoji]

———

HEBE: can you check on my plants at the flat? I'm thinking of extending my Europe trip.

HOLLY: you are NOT ALLOWED to move to Europe

HEBE: just a few more weeks, I promise

HEBE: I was thinking, though, about next year

> HOLLY: what next year? there's still so much this year, we are TOURING, Hebes. There's a bus and a bunch of awesome skeevy clubs across the country and when we get to Sydney there is ARENA SEATING and when I saw how many tickets they have sold already I did something that Juniper described as "swooning" but it might have actually been a stroke

HEBE: have you considered an international tour?

> HOLLY: hahahahaha

HEBE: ask Sage if he's aware how many hotels his boyfriend's mother owns, and get back to me

> HOLLY: ...
>
> HOLLY: brb

REAL UNREAL FM: Hey, so if you haven't been living under a rock, or trapped in an infinite mirror in the Shadowmancy department, you've heard of Fake Geek Girl. Since their third album dropped last year after an epic Witchstarter campaign, they're kind of everywhere. And they used to play every Friday night at Medea's Cauldron. Welcome to the studio, Holly, Juniper and Sage!

HOLLY: Glad to be here

SAGE: Not weird at all to be back on campus.

REAL UNREAL FM: so you have to be on the top ten list of Belladonna's most famous alumni!

JUNIPER: Really? Is there an official list? What criteria did they take into account?

REAL UNREAL FM: Since Like Witches For Coffee came out you've won three awards for this album, including the coveted Silver Siren for best Aussie indie single, and you've completed a national tour. What's next for Fake Geek Girl?

HOLLY: Europe, baby. The Tour goes on!

JUNIPER: We're delighted to have been invited to headline the Pied Piper festival in Germany. We're currently signing up guest instrumentalists from six different countries to join us on tour, including keyboards, the enchanted dulcimer, and the lute.

SAGE: Still no guitars. Got to draw the line somewhere.

REAL UNREAL FM: Any new songs on the horizon for the tour?

SAGE: It's too soon for a new album.

HOLLY: That's Sage's way of saying he's written three albums worth of songs already

SAGE: Holly Hallow is a liar. It's more like two and a half.

JUNIPER: We're always working on new material, but the tour is particularly to showcase the songs from Like Witches For Coffee.

HOLLY: It's a great album, we're really proud of it. Not ready to stop talking about it yet!

REAL UNREAL FM: So I have to ask this one, we do it whenever former students come back for an interview. How exactly did Belladonna U change your life?

[three seconds of dead air]

[all three members of the band start talking at the same time]

END

BONUS PLAYLISTS AND EXTRAS

PART ONE

PREVIOUS HITS

A FEW FAVES FROM FAKE GEEK GIRL: THE FIRST ALBUM &
RESTING WITCH FACE: THE AWKWARD SECOND ALBUM

GENERIC LOVE SONG (SOMETHING ABOUT SPOILERS)
BY FAKE GEEK GIRL

I love you so much that I care your favourite
*   show got cancelled*
Again
I care that they whitewashed the casting,
And queerbaited the fans
And they fridged three female lead characters one
*   after the other*
That really sucks
I'm so sorry
And something about spoilers

I love that you care that your game just isn't the
*   same without mirrors*
I love that you care that two fictional characters
*   who never kiss on the mouth might someday*
*   get married*
Or have a threesome
With that one guy whose name I can never
*   remember*
But he's totally in that other show that you love
Not the one that got cancelled

The other one
This is how much I love you
This is how much I care
I don't understand why you have to see the movie
      the first day it comes out even though the
      line's super long and it will be the exact same
      movie if you see it a week later
Because something about spoilers

I love you
And that's why I care
That the award went to the wrong writer
In fact all the awards are broken
And the reviewers are sexist
And you and your best friend are fighting
The best friend I've never met
Because she lives on the internet
And something about spoilers

I don't really care
But I love that you care
I love that you have a whole secret language of
      letters
OMG OTP OT3 WTF it all means something
      to you
Actually I'm pretty clear on WTF
We have that one in the real world too
I love you so much that I read a book with
      vampires in it
Even though they made a TV show about it and I
      could watch that instead
The book was quite terrible
But I'm reading the sequel
I won't ever tell you
Because I love that expression on your face

When I say I'm going to look up the ending on
    Wikipedia
I don't care about spoilers
But you really do

I love you
I love your thirty five fandoms
And your one true pairings
And your intense flamewars about pop culture
    analysis
And your games with imaginary friends
And the way you watch TV shows like someone is
    scoring points
(and maybe someday you'll win)
I love all these things about you
I don't really care
But I love that you care
And something about spoilers

STUPID SONGS ABOUT
VICTORIAN NOVELS
JUNIPER'S FIRST SOLO

I've never been in love
But I've read Victorian novels
And I'm not sure they're going to help me survive
If you break my heart
Then I'll send you a book list
Of girls who were broken
And are haunting me still

I've never been in love
But I've read Emily Bronte
And I know how this ends
So please let's not
Turn this into a ballad
Of lovers and screaming and wailing and
  haunting
Love stories like that
Are too hard on the heart

I write stupid songs about Victorian novels
Because someone has to be angry and anxious
About the girls who are broken

And die at the end

I once read a story
About a girl who was broken
And I thought she'd survive it
And build a new life
But the world was too harsh
And so was the writer
Don't trust Thomas Hardy
He'll crumble your dreams

I write stupid songs about Victorian novels
Because someone has to be burning with fury
About the girls who are broken
And die at the end

Don't get me started on the Mill on the Floss
I don't want to talk about the Mill on the Floss
I'm really not over the Mill on the Floss
George Eliot, I'm looking at you
And Dickens? Oh, Dickens, I'll damn you to hell
You know what you did, when you killed
    Little Nell
(Based on a real person, love)
(That doesn't make it better)

I've never been in love
But I've read Victorian novels
And I'm not sure they're going to help me survive
If you break my heart
Then I'll send you a book list
Of girls who were broken
And are haunting me still

I write stupid songs about Victorian novels

Because someone has to be angry and anxious
About the girls who are broken
And die at the end

I can only hope that those authors were haunted
By those poor souls that they sent on their way
Is it bad, is it wrong, is it strange that I'm crying
They're still breaking girls on the page to this day

Let them live one more time
Let them fight for their story
Let them torment their authors
Long past their own graves
Shout their names to the wind
On the moor as it darkens
And the storm closes in
Swim hard up the river
With the wind whipping madly
Let them haunt, let them haunt
Let the haunting begin

BURN HARD
WRITING CREDIT, SAGE MCCLAREN
- PERFORMED BY KRAKEN

I'm waiting in the car
For you to finish work
And I see the smoke before I see the flame
You're burning up my back seat with
Everything you did today
And I know this can go
One of two ways

Grind against me
Spark and tinder
I could talk you down
But I'm not that guy
I could damp your flame
But I wanna watch you fly
(right at my face)

You and I are an explosion waiting to happen
Don't wait
Light it up
Let's go

I set fire to your broom,
You'll incinerate my car,
Flame on,
This is us
Burn hard

Why try to pretend we don't like the sight
Of good things burning
Why try to pretend
We're better than this
I'm smoke
You're fire
The smell of burning tyres
Is just what I desire in a valentine

You and I are an explosion waiting to happen
Don't wait
Light it up
Let's go

I set fire to your broom,
You'll incinerate my car,
Flame on,
This is us
Burn hard

Light it up
Let's go
You're so hot
When I'm on fire
Don't wait
Light it up
This is us
Burn hard

PART TWO

LIKE WITCHES FOR COFFEE: THE ALBUM

- **Coffee is The Key To Surviving You** (vocals: Holly Hallow, lyrics: Sage McClaren)
- **Cryptids** (vocals: Holly, feat. Sofia the Belladonna U Lake Beast, lyrics: Holly)
- **Team Pandora** (vocals & lyrics: Sage)
- **Pockets** (vocals & lyrics: Juniper Cresswell)
- **Vex Me** (vocals: Holly, mystery pianist:?? lyrics: Holly & Juniper)
- **Cauldron Full of Cats** (vocals: Holly, sarcastic refrain: Sage, lyrics: Holly)
- **My T-Shirt's in Paris Now** (vocals & lyrics: Sage)
- **Everyone's Kissed the Drummer** (vocals & lyrics: Holly)
- **The Basilisk Song** (vocals: Sage & Holly, lyrics: Ferd Chauvelin, Hebe Hallow, Sage, Holly, Juniper)
- **My Love is a Cake Wizard** (vocals: Holly, Sage, Juniper, feat. Nora @ keyboards, lyrics: Holly)

WITCHSTARTER EXCLUSIVE BONUS TRACKS

- **Pockets** (vocals: Sage, feat. mystery pianist:?? & three drum solos)
- **Stupid Songs About Victorian Novels: Disco Mix** (vocals: Holly, feat. Nora on keyboards)
- **Witches Roll Dice, Bitches: Regency Ballroom Mix** (vocals: Juniper, feat. mystery harpist:??)

CAULDRON FULL OF CATS

No one wants to hear about happy ever after
You rescued the damsel
The princess is in your castle
Congratulations
(congratu-fucking-lations)
You got to the end
No one wants to hear that she's sweet in the
      mornings
Her hair is like honey
Her kisses like the last drop of wine
(You finished that whole bottle?)

They might want to hear about the dragons you
      fought off
The quests you completed
The big budget cut scene
The stats, oh the stats, good and bad, you can
      keep to yourself
They might even cheer that first time that she
      kissed you
(she's the brave one)

Against all the odds
They were pleased for you both
Game over, it's done
You totally won
But now it's got boring, you're nothing but happy
Her hair is like honey
Her kisses like the last bite of peach
(I was saving that, witch)

It was all so dramatic
For five or six minutes
But they take you for granted
Now you're in a pair
It's been months now
You're yesterday's news
Please don't text your friends to say
How great her hair smells
(No one cares)
They're not that invested
Please don't overshare

Your friends are all bored with your cottagecore
        romance
A cauldron full of cats and
Roses grown wild round the door
You overcame your shortcomings
And she overlooked all your flaws
They were sick of the pining but oh
This is so much worse
No one wants to hear that she's sweet in the
        mornings
Her hair is like honey
Her kisses the last breath of air

It's all so domestic

The cats need to be fed now
Please water the roses
And pour me one too
While you text your friends to share news like
"I can't believe she's still here"
They're not that invested
Please don't overshare

No one wants to hear you're my all and my
    darling
My always and maybe my only
High score everlasting
A cauldron full of cats and
Roses grown wild round the door
No one wants to hear us
Our late night sweet nothings as the screen runs
    to static
Secret smiles and a softness
That was never quite me
No one wants to hear that you're sweet in the
    mornings
Your hair is like honey
Your kisses like the last cup of coffee

The credits have rolled
The cats need to be be fed now
Please water the roses
And pour me one too
You're still holding my hand
*(*She's still holding your hand*)*
Game over, it's done
We totally won

THE BASILISK SONG

hello, how are you, I'm fine
I guess you are wondering what's on my mind
you look so familiar there across the room
and your name is on the tip of my tongue
you turn your head a touch too soon
and I swear the air punches right out of my lungs

you're the person I dated at uni
I still remember how you took your coffee
and how much you hated every citrus fruit
I know what tattoos are inked on your back
and I wonder when we stopped texting hello

because we stayed friends
that's the worst thing about it
friends aren't supposed to stop texting hello

we went through hell
I remember it well
and by the end I wasn't even sure that you
     liked me

but we stayed friends
that's the worst thing about it
friends aren't supposed to stop texting hello

let's catch up, pour a wine
how are your friends, how are mine?
no one's fault, such a shame
we lost touch, I guess it happens
and I really wish I could remember your name

your eyes still shine and I
still love your smile
and by the end I wasn't even sure that you
      liked me
but we stayed friends
that's the worst thing about it
friends aren't supposed to stop texting hello

we were star-cross'd lovers
and nothing stood between us
we fought for our love and we won
our friends came around
and my house burned to the ground
the world tried to break us and we still didn't
      shatter
I held your hand
you led me through the burning rubble
look at it all, we survived to fight the monsters
basilisks fell before us and we found our way
      back home

and by the end I wasn't even sure that you
      liked me
but we stayed friends

that's the worst thing about it
friends aren't supposed to stop texting hello

I hate that you wrote this
I hate you saw our future
and I really wish I could remember your name

CRYPTIDS

Am I invisible
Or is this what the future holds
I'm a voice in the walls
I'm an hourly rate
I think I forgot
How I got in this state

Unicorns don't need day jobs
Bigfoot doesn't have paperwork to file
Bunyips don't need to pay rent on their caves
Let's run away together and live in a hole in the
*   ground*
I'll keep you warm
And you keep me grounded
Let's run away together and live in a hole in the
*   ground*

We used to be outrageous
We were mythical beasts
We shouted onstage
We played beautiful music

We raged and we stormed, we were lightning and
    earthquakes

Now I'm invisible
I turn up each morning, I do what I'm told
I miss you, love
I never even kissed you, was I out of my mind?
If you come back
Can we run away together and live in a hole in
    the ground
(No one will ever find us)

We used to be outrageous
We were cryptids together
We shouted onstage
We played beautiful music
We raged and we stormed, we were lightning and
    earthquakes

I forgot how to be a beautiful creature
But if I find your hiding spot, I think you'll
    remind me
I'll quit my day job
We'll be cryptids forever
Let's run away together and live in a hole in the
    ground

POCKETS

I saw a girl out walking with a
Beautiful smile
and she said: "I like your dress"
I replied: "Thanks, it has pockets"
Then I realised really quickly
What she'd actually said:
She'd said: "I like your face"
And I'd said: "Thanks, it has pockets"
And that's a whole different conversation
But I was in too deep to turn around

Do you like my smile?
It has pockets
I contain multitudes
Do you like my hair?
It has pockets
So much storage space for secrets
Do you like my song?
It's full of pockets
That's why it came out kind of wrong
Please don't try to sing along

This is the pocket song

I saw a girl out walking with a
Knowing look
and she asked me: what ya reading?
And I meant to say: a book
But instead I was still thinking
About my pretty dress
And I said: "Thanks, it has pockets"
You don't need to tell me I'm a mess
(we all noticed, love)
(I thought you might)

Do you like my eyes?
They have pockets
I have not been sleeping well
Do you like my shoes
They have pockets
It's not as comfortable as you might think
Do you like my song?
It's full of pockets
(So many freaking pockets)
That's why it came out kind of wrong
Please don't try to sing along
I've laid traps along the way
(You'll trip and fall)

I took my girl out walking
We were strolling in the snow
She said: "I like your crazy thoughts"
And I tried to say: "I know"
But I replied: "Thanks, they have pockets"
And she said: "I'm well aware"
"That must come in sort of handy"
And I said: "Well, here and there"

And then I said, "Hang on, I think I'm wearing
 your dress, actually..."
And she said:

[with _AUDIENCE:_]
Thanks, it has pockets

Do you like my smile?
It has pockets
I contain multitudes
Do you like my hair?
It has pockets
So much storage space for secrets
Do you like my song?
It's full of pockets
Told you not to sing along
I laid traps inside my song
(You tripped and fell into her pockets)
(So far down)
And it's here that you belong
Down deep inside my pockets
Nothing to see here, move along

MY T-SHIRT'S IN PARIS NOW

My best t-shirt's in Paris now
I know you are to blame
It couldn't be my fault (you didn't say goodbye)
I emptied your suitcase and I shouted your name
But you still managed to leave
I don't know where you are
but I hope my t-shirt keeps you warm
Send me a fucking postcard, tell me when you're
      coming home

I said, don't go
Be my friend, stay at home
don't steal my fucking t-shirts just to keep a piece
      of me
your place is here
just here
there's a room waiting for you
if you had to leave, couldn't you take me too?

Who even goes to Paris?
It can't be a real place

If you have to fly to get there then it seems too
*   far away*
You said growing up was a race you had to win
that means moving forward
away from everything you love
you just left
(you had to leave)
I don't know where you are
but I hope my t-shirt keeps you warm
Send me a fucking postcard, tell me when you're
*   coming home*

I said don't fly
clip your wings, stay at home
who came up with that bullshit line about loving,
*   letting go*
your place is here
just here
there's a room waiting for you
if you had to leave, couldn't you take me too?

My worst friend is in Paris now,
She left me standing here
Croissants and wine can't be that great
Do they even have good beer?
I don't know where you are but I hope my t-shirt
*   keeps you warm*
Send me a fucking postcard, tell me when you're
*   coming home*

(I'll buy so many t-shirts you can steal when you
*   come home)*

COFFEE IS THE KEY TO
SURVIVING YOU

I'm allergic to your smile
& I'm pretty sure this is gonna kill me
Still, stay a while
(a while)
I'm almost getting used to the watering eyes
Don't say you love me
Your magic is crawling under my skin (my skin)
& I don't think you understand
What a bloody awful nightmare situation we
    are in

My blood is freezing
I think my heart stopped beating an hour ago
You're being so nice to me
(so nice to me)
But your magic wants me dead
& to be honest your mother might too
Your mouth on mine was a terrible idea
Your hand in mine is a hell of a sight
Pour a cup of coffee, love
& maybe the two of us will live through this night

(you'll survive me)
(I'll survive you)
let's get through this night

You're allergic to my smile
& I'm pretty sure this is gonna kill you
Still, stay a while
(a while)
I left bloody scorchmarks all down your spine
Don't let me love you
My magic is crawling under your skin
(so much skin)
& I don't think you understand
What a bloody awful fucked up
nightmare of a situation we are in

Your skin is burning
I think your brain stopped functioning an
*   hour ago*
I'm being so fucking nice to you
(nice and easy...)
But my magic wants you dead
& to be honest my best friend might too
Your mouth on mine was a terrible idea
Your hand in mine is a hell of a sight
Pour a cup of coffee, love
& maybe the two of us will live through this night

If there's enough coffee in that pot
(enough coffee)
I'm pretty sure the two of us will live through this
*   night*
(you'll survive me)
(I'll survive you)
let's get through this night

ABOUT THE AUTHOR

Tansy Rayner Roberts is an award-winning Australian science fiction and fantasy author who owns far too pointy hats. She had a great time at university.

- What tea is Tansy drinking? Find out when you subscribe to her excellent newsletter
- Listen to Tansy on Sheep Might Fly, a podcast where she reads aloud her stories as audio serials. The Belladonna U series started here!
- Read Tansy's stories before anyone else when you pledge to her Patreon: patreon.com/tansyrr
- Follow Tansy on Amazon or Bookbub so you never miss a release.

facebook.com/TansyRRoberts
twitter.com/tansyrr
instagram.com/tansyrr

ALSO BY
TANSY RAYNER ROBERTS

Thanks so much for reading! Please consider leaving a review or star rating, to help other readers find me.

Sign up to my newsletter for free stories and more:

https://tinyurl.com/tansyrr

You can hear many of my stories first on the Sheep Might Fly podcast.

Check out my other books:

Unreal Alchemy

Holiday Brew

Castle Charming

Gate Sinister

House Perilous

Gorgons Deserve Nice Things

Musketeer Space

Joyeux

Merry Happy Valkyrie

Tea & Sympathetic Magic

The Frost Fair Affair

Spellcracker's Honeymoon

Lady Liesl's Seaside Surprise

Have Spirit, Will Duchess

Power & Majesty

The Shattered City

Reign of Beasts

Cabaret of Monsters

NON-FICTION & ESSAYS

From Baby Brain to Writer Brain: Writing Through A World Of
Parenting Distractions

It's Raining Musketeers

Pratchett's Women: Unauthorised Essays

AS EDITOR

Mother of Invention (with Rivqa Rafael)

Cranky Ladies of History (with Tehani Croft)